™

*My name is Kara Zor-El. When I was a child, my planet, Krypton, was dying. I was sent to Earth to protect my cousin, but my pod got knocked off course, and by the time I got here, my cousin had already grown up and become Superman. I hid who I really was until one day when an accident forced me to reveal myself to the world.*

*To most people, I'm Kara Danvers, a reporter at CatCo Worldwide Media. But in secret, I work with my adoptive sister, Alex, for the Department of Extra-Normal Operations to protect my city from alien life and anyone else that means to cause it harm. I am . . .*

# RGIRL™

## AGE OF ATLANTIS

BY JO WHITTEMORE

AMULET BOOKS
NEW YORK

## TO MY HUSBAND, ARI,
## WHO IS MY FAVORITE SUPERHERO

The Library of Congress has cataloged the hardcover edition as follows:
Names: Whittemore, Jo, 1977– author.
Title: Supergirl: age of Atlantis / by Jo Whittemore.
Other titles: Supergirl (Television program)
Description: New York: Amulet Books, 2017. | Series: Supergirl; [1]
Identifiers: LCCN 2017031640 | ISBN 9781419728143 (hardback)
Subjects: | BISAC: JUVENILE FICTION / Action & Adventure / General. |
JUVENILE FICTION / Media Tie-In.
Classification: LCC PZ7.W617828 Sup 2017 | DDC [Fic]—dc23
Paperback ISBN 978-1-4197-3609-4

Supergirl based on characters created by Jerry Siegel and Joe Shuster.
By special arrangement with the Jerry Siegel family.

ABBO39359

Originally published in hardcover by Amulet Books in 2017
Cover illustration by César Moreno
Book design by Chad W. Beckerman

Printed and bound in U.S.A.
11 10 9 8 7 6 5 4 3

Amulet Books are available at special discounts when purchased in quantity for premiums and promotions as well as fundraising or educational use. Special editions can also be created to specification. For details, contact specialsales@abramsbooks.com or the address below.

Amulet Books® is a registered trademark of Harry N. Abrams, Inc.

**ABRAMS** The Art of Books
195 Broadway, New York, NY 10007
abramsbooks.com

# 1

B RRRRING!

*BEEP! BEEP! BEEP!*

"*. . . traffic on the interstate . . .*"

Monday morning.

All across National City, people were waking and stretching to their alarm clocks. But one National City resident relied on a slightly different alarm clock: her superhearing.

"*Everyone on the floor NOW! Purses and wallets out, or I start shooting!*"

Kara Danvers opened her eyes and sat up in bed.

Bank robbers.

And they couldn't even wait until after she'd had her morning coffee.

She tilted her head and listened for other sounds to help

her locate the robbery. Squawking parrots and barking dogs placed it near a pet store, and she could hear carousel music from Pineda Park. That narrowed the crime down to one location.

"National City Bank and Trust," Kara said, hopping out of bed.

In ten seconds, she was smoothing down her red skirt and cape as her alter ego, Supergirl. In ten more seconds, she'd touched down on the sidewalk outside the bank.

Supergirl narrowed her eyes and used her X-ray vision to see through the stone facade into . . . an empty lobby.

Yet she could hear weeping and frightened whispers.

Scanning the building's interior more closely, she spotted a floor-to-ceiling vault in the corner. Its door was open, blocking her view of its contents, and the entire structure was made of lead—something her X-ray vision couldn't penetrate. But Supergirl had no doubt the thieves and hostages were hiding inside.

Pedestrians hurried past the bank, absorbed in their busy lives and oblivious to the panic Supergirl could hear through the walls. There was no reason to spread chaos to the street, so she strolled up to the bank's entrance and tried the front door. Several passersby slowed their pace, giving her curious looks.

"I need a loan for a new spaceship," she said with a smile.

The passersby regarded her with wide eyes, and inwardly, Supergirl regretted the joke. She could already see the *National City Tribune* headline: *Supergirl Broke! Next Stop: The Soup-er Kitchen?*

With a sigh, she tugged at the door handle, but felt no give.

*Locked from the inside*, she thought.

Supergirl twisted the handle until the metal groaned and the lock popped out of place. The door swung open and she stepped inside, relocking the door behind her.

On featherlight feet, the Girl of Steel crept around wallets and purses that had been strewn across the floor, counting them as she did so. At least fifteen hostages.

Voices echoed off the far wall, coming from inside the vault.

"I already told you, I can't open the deposit boxes!" said a woman's shaking voice. "The locks are fingerprint-activated, so only the box holders can open them."

A man snorted. "That's a lie. There has to be an override."

"Yeah," said another man. "Otherwise," he added in a menacing voice, "what happens when someone loses their fingers?"

Someone whimpered, and a child started to cry.

That was more than enough. Supergirl had to end this—but the vault was too crowded for her to risk charging in. She needed to flush the robbers *and* the hostages out of hiding.

Supergirl glanced up and saw fire sprinklers dotting the lobby ceiling. Surely, the vault had sprinklers, too.

She found a mirror among the discarded purses and flew across the room, landing softly behind the open vault door. Holding the mirror at eye level, Supergirl tilted it until she could see inside the vault. There were sixteen hostages, two thuggish robbers, and . . . a sprinkler.

Aiming the mirror at the sprinkler, Supergirl fixed her gaze on the reflective surface. A second later, neon-blue beams of thermal energy shot from her eyes and struck the mirror. The mirror, in turn, bounced the heated beams at the sprinkler inside the vault.

Hissing and sputtering, the sprinkler unleashed a miniature rain shower. With surprised shouts, the hostages fled the vault, the robbers following close behind. None of them noticed Supergirl as she did a quick head count—but they all noticed when the three-ton vault door slammed shut and she leaned against it.

"The weather in here sure is unpredictable, isn't it?" she asked.

At the sight of Supergirl, the hostages' expressions went from downtrodden to uplifted. They whispered her name in excited voices and hugged one another.

Her appearance had the opposite effect on the robbers.

"It's Supergirl! Run!" cried the first robber.

"Superwho?" asked the second, glancing at his partner. Or, rather, at the place where his partner had been standing.

Robber 1 had dropped a bag of money and taken his own advice, dashing toward one of the exits. Supergirl considered chasing him, but she couldn't leave the hostages. Plus, Robber 2 would likely rat out his partner for a reduced prison sentence.

"You must be new in town," Supergirl told Robber 2 with a smile. "Why don't we talk at the police station?"

Supergirl took a step toward him, and the robber pointed a lump in his jacket pocket at her. "Stand back! I've got a gun and I'll shoot everyone in here!"

Several of the hostages screamed.

Supergirl squinted at the robber's jacket, her X-ray vision passing through the flimsy nylon to see a clenched— but empty—hand in his pocket.

"You don't have a gun. You have a *fist*," she corrected, closing the distance between them. "And guess what? So do I."

The robber's eyes widened as Supergirl's arm reeled back.

"You might want to close 'em for this," she said.

Then she knocked him across the room.

The hostages cheered, and Supergirl gave them a smile

and a wave before zipping out the bank doors. She wished she could've stayed until the police arrived, but she was already late to meet her sister, Alex.

Supergirl flew across town and dipped low over the roof of Noonan's restaurant, scooping up a change of clothes she'd stowed there. One of the downsides to her superhero outfit? No pockets.

She landed behind Noonan's and, making sure she was alone, quickly pulled on the clothes she wore as Kara Danvers. As she stepped into a pair of red flats, she smiled, wondering what her coworkers would think if she showed up in red Supergirl boots instead. Since Kara dressed conservatively to hide her true identity, she'd no doubt be the talk of the office.

From the left pocket of her slacks, Kara pulled her lead-lined eyeglasses, and from the right pocket her cell phone, which flashed with a message from Alex.

*My coffee's getting cold, and I don't have heat vision.*

Kara chuckled and picked up her red boots. With a flick of the wrist, she tossed them onto Noonan's roof and then hurried to the entrance of the restaurant. She skidded to a stop just inside, spotting a familiar freckle-faced, auburn-haired woman in line.

Alex's coffee wasn't getting cold. She hadn't even ordered yet!

"It's not nice to lie to family," Kara said, bumping her sister.

Alex shot Kara a wry smile and put an arm around her. "I figured pity was the quickest way to get you here." She held up a finger. "By the way, if you're this late when your boss needs you, no wonder he's grouchy."

Alex was talking about Snapper Carr, Kara's boss at CatCo Worldwide Media, where Kara worked as a reporter. At least . . . when she could get her stories printed. Her boss still didn't treat her like a full-fledged member of the team. Last week, she'd let the mayor cancel an interview, and Snapper had called Kara "Glasses McPushover."

At least it was a change from "Ponytail."

Kara's recent work problems were the reason she'd asked Alex to meet at Noonan's that morning, and as Alex commented on her tardiness, Kara rolled her eyes.

"It's not like I'm late because I overslept," said Kara. "I was stopping a bank robbery."

The guy in front of them glanced back at her.

"In a video game I was playing," Kara added with a nervous laugh.

He faced forward again, and Alex pinched her sister's arm.

"Your inside voice needs an inside voice!" Alex whispered.

Alex was right, of course, but maintaining a secret identity was hard work. Kara hated always having guarded conversations—never knowing who was listening or watching. She loved being a superhero, though sometimes she wished it didn't make her such an oddity.

The guy in front of them finished placing his order, and Alex and Kara stepped up to the counter. A shaggy-haired college kid with a name tag that read MARCUS greeted them.

"Hi!" said Kara. "Can I get a spiced pumpkin with extra foam and just a little bit of sprinkles on top, please?"

"You got it." Marcus poised a pen over Kara's cup. "What's your name, pretty lady?"

Alex rolled her eyes and Kara ducked her head and snickered, tucking her hair behind her ear.

"Who, me?"

Alex put a hand on her sister's shoulder. "Her name's Kara."

"Nice name!" said Marcus. "Carla." He wrote as he spoke.

Kara cleared her throat. "Actually, it's Kara. With a *K* and no *L*."

"Whoops! My bad." Marcus crossed out what he'd written and scribbled the new name. "Better?"

The cup now read . . . CARKA.

Alex turned her head and stifled a laugh while Kara forced a smile.

"Close enough," she said. "Can I also get some doughnuts to go?"

Marcus passed the cup to the barista and grabbed a pastry box, loading it with Kara's favorite flavors. Which was pretty much everything except maple logs.

"You know what? Throw a maple log in there, too," she said as Marcus started to close the pastry box. At a raised eyebrow from Alex, she explained, "For Snapper."

Alex snorted. "Kara, no amount of food is going to make Snapper a nice person."

Kara sighed. "If you have any better ideas, I'm all ears."

"You need to speak his language," Alex told her.

"I do! Every time Snapper's mean to me, I'm just as mean back."

Alex leaned against the counter, arms crossed. "All right, I'll bite. What's a typical Kara Danvers insult?"

Kara inclined her head. "Just last week, he told me my grammar sucked, and I told *him* that"—Kara adjusted her glasses—"that he'd missed a button on his shirt." She swiped at some spilled sugar on the counter. "So . . . he was probably pret-ty embarrassed."

Alex laughed and hugged her younger sister. "Sweetie, being mean just isn't you. And that's not what I meant by 'speak his language.' People like Snapper want big. Bold." She shrugged. "They want attention."

"Big. Bold." Kara repeated to herself, nodding. "I can do that!"

But ten minutes later, as Kara rode the CatCo elevator to the twentieth floor, no big *or* bold ideas had come to her. She'd have to wing it when she reached Snapper's desk. The elevator doors opened, and she took a deep breath before she stepped out.

Snapper, a scowling Latino man with a fringe of dark hair, was reviewing a layout with an equally annoyed-looking black man—one of Kara's closest friends, James Olsen. At one time, James had been a photographer at the *Daily Planet*, where Kara's cousin Clark Kent worked, but Clark had then sent James to National City to watch over Kara.

James was one of the few people who knew that Clark Kent was Superman and Kara Danvers, Supergirl. Now James was the acting CEO at CatCo, which meant butting heads with section leaders so much he was constantly rubbing his shaved scalp in frustration . . . or pain.

Snapper and James spoke a few words to each other, and then Snapper picked up the layout and carried it back to his desk. Kara hurried forward, but before she could speak, Snapper cupped his hands around his mouth and shouted across the newsroom floor.

"Investigative journos at my desk!"

Kara pointed to herself and smiled. "Is there a prize for being the first one here?"

Snapper scowled at her. "Danvers, this meeting isn't for you."

Kara's smile dipped a little. "Uh . . . you wanted to see the investigative journalists, and I'm one of them."

"You are?!" Snapper's eyes widened in mock surprise. "Great! I'll take that interview with Mayor Lowell." He held out his hand, palm up.

It took immense willpower for Kara not to grab Snapper's wrist and flip him over her shoulder.

"He canceled, remember?" She spoke in as even a voice as she could muster. "I don't have the interview."

Snapper pointed to the elevator. "Then don't come back until you do."

"You're not serious."

Snapper's finger didn't waver. "Hit the pavement, Danvers. I want that interview."

Kara chanced a glimpse at James in case he might be able to step in, but he was focused on a cluster of television screens in his office. Clenching her fists by her side, Kara turned on her heel and stalked back toward the elevator, pushing the down button so hard the panel sunk into the wall. With a guilty glance around, she tucked her hands behind her back.

Now, instead of thinking, *Big. Bold*, Kara thought, *Totally. Doomed*, all the way down.

# 2

EVEN THOUGH CATCO WAS JUST A few blocks from City Hall, Kara was sweating by the time she reached her destination.

She'd never met the mayor before. Not as Kara Danvers, anyway. And it was different when she was Supergirl. When she put on that costume, she also put on extra courage.

Wiping her sweaty palms on her slacks, Kara opened the front door and smiled at the security guards on either side. She passed through the metal detector and approached the information desk, where a woman with a perfectly coiffed updo sat perfectly upright with her hands perfectly folded in front of her. The placard on her desk read ZELDA BINDER.

"Welcome to City Hall!" she chirped, following her greeting with a wide smile. "How may I help you?"

"I'm here to see the mayor?" Kara chided herself for making it sound like a question. "I mean, I'm here to see the mayor. I'm with CatCo Worldwide Media." She held up her ID badge.

"CatCo?" Ms. Binder glanced at something on her desk. "I'm sorry, but Mayor Lowell's unavailable for the foreseeable future." She smiled indulgently again, but something flickered across her face. Something that looked a lot like guilt.

Kara studied the woman. "Was he unavailable *before* I mentioned who I worked for?"

The wide smile tightened. "Is there anything else I can help you with, hon?" Ms. Binder reached into her desk and pulled out a rolled-up stack of glossy pages. "How about a National City calendar?"

*Does it have dates when the mayor's free?* Kara wanted to ask. Instead, she took the calendar and gave a polite nod. "Thank you for your time."

"My pleasure. Have a lovely day!" Ms. Binder chirped as Kara walked away.

As she left the building, Kara tapped the rolled calendar against her palm. She couldn't go back to CatCo because she hadn't interviewed the mayor, and she couldn't interview the mayor because, well . . . she had no idea why. Whatever the reason, she had a feeling it had to do specifically with CatCo. She pulled out her phone and texted James:

*Any idea why Mayor Lowell hates CatCo?*

As soon as she sent it, she received an automatic reply:

*Guardian mode.*

Kara swore under her breath. Being friends with Superman and Supergirl had inspired James to become a hero of his own: Guardian. But because he was a human with no innate powers or defenses, he'd recruited Kara's other best friend (and mechanical genius), Winn Schott, for help. Ever the inventor, Winn had made James a twenty-first-century knight's helmet and lead-lined, padded body armor with a deployable shield built into one arm.

Usually Guardian fought crime at night, with Winn monitoring remotely, so if they were patrolling in broad daylight, they must be really bored. Kara hated the idea of her two friends putting their lives in danger, but she couldn't stop them, so she usually just hoped for the best and did something to distract herself.

Like call her boyfriend, Mon-El.

"Hey! How's my favorite Kryptonian?" Mon-El asked when he answered the phone.

Kara grinned and skipped down the last couple of steps outside City Hall. "Good. What's my favorite Daxamite up to?"

"I'm at the museum," said Mon-El.

"The museum? Are you lost?" Kara teased.

As the former playboy prince of the planet Daxam, Mon-El hadn't exactly been the studious type.

"Ha ha," he said, but Kara could hear the smile in his voice. "For your information, I'm trying to improve my knowledge of humans, so I thought I'd start with Neanderthals and work my way up."

"Impressive!" said Kara. "Could you use some company?"

"Always," said Mon-El. "But don't you have work?"

Kara made a face. "Not so much."

As she walked to the museum, she told Mon-El about her morning and her confusing encounter at City Hall.

"That *is* weird," he said when Kara finished. "Has CatCo published anything negative about the mayor lately?"

"Not that I know of." Kara paid the museum attendant and wandered into the first hall. "Where are you?" she asked Mon-El.

"With the Ancient Romans. Did you know they used to sacrifice sheep in apology to the gods?" Kara saw Mon-El gazing up at a statue in the Roman wing. "On Daxam, we just sang the apology song."

She laughed and Mon-El turned, his dark eyes brightening at the sight of her. She gave him a quick kiss and held the calendar out to him.

"I brought you a present. It's a City Hall calendar."

"Well, way to spoil the surprise." Mon-El unfurled it. "'A Year of Civic Initiatives.' And this month's is digital libraries!" He put a hand to his heart. "You are a true romantic, Kara Zor-El," he said, using her Kryptonian name.

Kara blushed and laughed. "Hey, I'll bet it's a gift no girl has ever gotten you."

"It is," he said, pulling her close.

"You don't have to keep it," she said with a smile.

"Thank you." Mon-El dropped the calendar where he stood.

Kara laughed. "You do have to throw it away, though."

"Right," he said, tossing it in a nearby trash can.

Kara glanced around at the Roman statues and pottery. "How is ancient history going to help you with modern humans, exactly?"

"Oh, I already understand way more about them," said Mon-El. "Like why they collect cat poop in those little boxes." At a confused look from Kara, he added, "Over in the Egyptian hall, I learned that cats are magical, so I'm thinking humans keep their waste for something. Probably energy drinks."

Kara pressed her lips together. "Maybe we should spend a little more time in the Egyptian hall."

*BANG!*

A gunshot echoed through the Roman wing. Kara and Mon-El both flinched.

Another gunshot reverberated off the walls, followed by a scream.

Kara stepped away from Mon-El. "I'm gonna change into something more comfortable."

"Yep," he said, cracking his neck and stretching his arms.

He might not have a superhero name, but since Daxam and Krypton were sister planets, Mon-El derived powers from Earth's sun just like Supergirl.

And it *had* been at least a week since he'd punched someone through a wall.

While Kara dashed off to become Supergirl, Mon-El ran toward the source of the chaos. In a room off the Roman wing, a security guard lay unconscious on the floor, gun still clutched in one hand. Unconcerned, a man and woman in street clothes were shattering display cases with wrenches.

"Now, now. Those tools are for fixing, not breaking," Mon-El said, crossing his arms.

With a *whoosh!* Supergirl was by his side. Both crooks finally stopped their display case destruction.

Supergirl scoffed at the male crook. "You again! Are you gonna bail on this partner, too?"

Mon-El glanced from her to the man. "You know him?"

"Yeah, he tried to rob a bank this morning but ran when he saw me." Supergirl smirked at the crook and leaned forward, splaying her fingers. "Boo."

This time, though, the man didn't run. Instead he smiled, the corners of his mouth bulging.

And bulging.

And bulging.

His cheeks swelled and when he parted his lips a high-pitched buzzing filled the air.

A second later, hundreds of bees launched from his mouth.

Supergirl's eyes widened and she stepped back. "OK, this morning he was *not* a bee breather."

"Bee Breather. Love the name," said Mon-El, "kinda hate the guy. But it's not like they can hurt us, right? Our skin's impervious to—OW!" A lone bee had settled on his hand and stabbed him with its stinger.

"Something tells me these aren't ordinary bees," Supergirl said, clenching her jaw.

The man snapped his fingers, and the swarm surrounded Supergirl and Mon-El in a dome of yellow and black.

The trapped twosome shifted closer together until they stood back-to-back.

"Mon-El?" Supergirl squeezed his hand. "If you're allergic to bees, now's the time to say so."

# 3

BEE BREATHER SNAPPED HIS fingers again, and with an angry buzz, the bees dove inward and downward, their stingers pointed at Supergirl and Mon-El.

"Duck!" Supergirl shouted, grabbing a corner of her cape and pulling it over her body. She spun toward Mon-El, who did as she asked, and Supergirl's cape enveloped them both.

But not completely. Their left sides were still exposed, and the bees changed their flight path to attack the vulnerable area.

Taking a deep breath, Supergirl turned her head toward the bees and exhaled a torrent of frosty air. Frozen solid, the tiny bee corpses clattered to the marble floor like hail on glass.

"No!" cried Bee Breather.

Mon-El pounded a fist into the tile beneath him, break-ing off a sizable piece. He hurled it across the room like a twenty-pound discus, aiming for Bee Breather's legs. The tile fragment knocked Bee Breather off his feet, and he fell—hard. His eyes slid shut, and the remaining bees flitted off in various directions.

Mon-El stood with a triumphant grin. "Talk about a buzzkill."

Supergirl didn't crack a smile. "Let's not celebrate yet." She nodded to Bee Breather's partner, who arched an eye-brow and smirked.

"Wise decision," said the woman. She raised her hands by her sides and wiggled her fingers.

Shards of broken glass from the display cases rattled and clinked against the floor before slowly lifting into the air. As they hovered, each piece rotated until its sharpest point faced Supergirl and Mon-El. The woman thrust her hands forward, and the slivers of glass sliced through the air toward the heroes.

Supergirl leaped in front of Mon-El, cape raised, but while she could stop the penetration of the glass, she couldn't stop the force behind it.

She and Mon-El were thrown across the room into a statue of Emperor Caligula. Supergirl grappled with the statue as it fell, but her fingers couldn't find purchase, and the ancient artifact smashed to the ground.

"Oops," said the female thief, putting a hand to her smiling lips. She raised the other hand and pointed at Mon-El. "You know, I haven't tried to levitate anything big yet."

With a twirl of her finger, the woman sent Mon-El airborne, lifting him higher and higher.

"I love vaulted ceilings," said Lady Levitation. "What would you say this is? Thirty, maybe forty feet?"

"Enough!" said Supergirl. Fist outstretched, she charged through the air toward the female thief, who lifted a hand in a halting gesture.

Supergirl felt a brief resistance, but controlling both heroes was too much for Lady Levitation, and Supergirl broke through. Just as her fist was about to connect with Lady Levitation's face, the thief nodded past Supergirl.

"Shouldn't you be more worried about him?"

Supergirl turned to see the invisible force lifting Mon-El let him go.

"Mon-El!" she shouted, dashing over.

Mon-El yelped as he fell but twisted his body in midair, landing on his feet with a ground-shaking thud.

"I'm all right," he told Supergirl. "But our friends are gone."

Supergirl whirled around to face a room full of relics, one unconscious security guard, and no crooks.

Sirens sounded nearby, and she could hear footsteps rushing from the other room.

"I have to get to the DEO," she told Mon-El. "Can you stay and handle this?"

He glanced around. "You mean explain how we destroyed a piece of history and only have a pile of dead bees to show for it?" Mon-El gave her a thumbs-up. "I love a challenge."

Supergirl gave him a quick kiss on the cheek and flew toward the exit. Behind her, she heard Mon-El tell someone, "We're really sorry about this. Could I interest you in a sacrificial sheep or apology song?"

As Supergirl sped toward the Department of Extra-Normal Operations, she scanned the ground for any sign of the museum thieves. No luck.

Zipping onto the balcony of the DEO control room, she took the stairs down two at a time, stopping when she reached the stone floor where the DEO insignia stretched before her. At the far end, J'onn J'onzz, the DEO's director, was drying his arms and face with a towel while he watched the screens on a video wall.

"Oh, good! The DEO got a pool," Supergirl said with a smirk. "I always thought this place could use something fun."

"We didn't get a pool," J'onn said calmly.

"And if we were going to get *anything* fun, I've already put in a request for a virtual reality room," Winn Schott spoke up from one of the desks surrounding the video wall.

Not long ago, he'd been a one-man IT department at CatCo. His friendship with Kara and his amazing tech skills had earned him a new job at the DEO.

J'onn faced Winn with a frown. "Why do you need virtual reality when you have actual reality?"

"Why . . . ?" Winn blinked at him and leaned forward. "J'onn, in virtual reality you can do *anything*. You can go to Hawaii or drive a Ferrari or beat up the kid who called you Cheap Schott when you ate a sandwich out of the trash . . ."

Supergirl and J'onn stared at him blankly.

"Or, you know. You could use it to see Mars."

J'onn pointed to Winn's keyboard. "Get back to your search."

Supergirl nodded approvingly. "So you're already working on the Bee Breather thing?"

J'onn and Winn both looked at her.

"What Bee Breather?" asked J'onn.

Before Supergirl could explain, Alex trotted over. In addition to being Kara's sister, she was J'onn's second-in-command at the DEO.

"Oh, good! I'm glad you're here," Alex told Supergirl. "Did J'onn and Winn brief you?"

Supergirl shook her head. "I actually came to tell you guys something."

Alex beckoned for her to follow. "Me first. There's something—er—some*one* you need to see."

J'onn handed Supergirl the damp towel. "You might need this."

Supergirl raised an eyebrow, but followed J'onn and Alex down a hallway to where the DEO held extra-normal criminals.

"Sorry to be so abrupt, but it's been a weird morning," Alex said.

Supergirl snorted. "You're telling me. The thief I chased out of the bank earlier suddenly has superpowers."

"What?" Alex stopped outside a cell with a sign that read PRISONER 52 above the door.

"Are you sure he didn't always have powers?" asked J'onn. "Maybe he was testing you this morning."

"He almost peed himself when he ran away," Supergirl said with a chuckle. "Trust me: He didn't have powers."

Alex placed her hand on a scanner to open Prisoner 52's door. "Well, we can help you with that if you can help us with this." She and J'onn stepped inside; wavy blue light shone across their faces.

Supergirl joined them and gaped in awe at the source. A massive aquarium tank dominated the room, water sloshing at its brim.

"You don't want to know how long it took to fill that thing," said Alex.

Inside the tank floated a humanoid creature with dark green flesh and webbing between its toes and fingers. Its torso appeared rubbery and bumpy like a frog's, and it had two tiny nostrils that produced bubbles every minute or so. Its mouth was massive, as were its eyes, which sized up Supergirl as she approached the tank.

"Who is this guy?" asked Supergirl. "I mean, I assume it's a guy."

"We think so, too," said J'onn. "But that's about all we can figure out. We hoped it might be an alien race you could identify."

Supergirl walked around the tank, the creature treading water in a circle to keep up with her.

"I'm sorry, but he's not any species I ever learned about." She tore her gaze away from the creature and looked at J'onn and Alex. "Where did you find him?"

"National City Aquarium." Alex pulled a tablet computer from a holster on the wall and showed the screen to Supergirl. On it was a video of the deep-sea exhibit at the aquarium. A crowd of people stood in a room below the water level where they could see inside the tank. Brightly patterned fish and stoic turtles swam around a scuba diver who was intermittently waving to the audience and feeding the animals. A dark figure swam toward the scuba diver, and the audience pointed to it and waved, assuming it was another diver.

Until the dark figure entered a patch of artificial light.

The crowd screamed at the face Supergirl recognized from the tank beside her: Prisoner 52. And he had no interest in waving to the audience or feeding the animals.

He just wanted to kill the scuba diver.

Supergirl clapped a hand to her mouth as Prisoner 52 tackled the scuba diver around the middle and proceeded to pummel him.

"That goes on for a few minutes before aquarium security figures out what to do," said Alex, closing the video. "Oddly, when our friend here was captured, he didn't try to attack anyone else. He did, however, try to speak." Alex pulled up a sound file that, to Supergirl's ears, was nothing more than screeches and squeaks. But out of the corner of her eye, Supergirl saw Prisoner 52 react.

"At least he recognizes his own voice," said Supergirl as Prisoner 52 swam side to side, water spilling over the top of his tank and onto the floor. "Since you can't figure out his species, I'm guessing you can't figure out his language?" she asked her sister.

"We've tried everything," said Alex. With a smirk, she added, "Winn even ran it through Google Translate."

Supergirl looked at J'onn. "What about telepathy?"

J'onn maintained the human appearance of Hank Henshaw, a black man in his fifties, but the DEO director was actually a Green Martian, capable of flight, shape-shifting, amazing strength, and mental communication.

He shook his head. "Nothing intelligible. Just random images of scuba divers."

Supergirl took the tablet from her sister and brought it closer to the tank, replaying the sound file for Prisoner 52. She pointed at him. "You. This is you."

The sea creature tilted his head and squawked, but didn't act as if he understood.

"We've already tried that," said Alex. "For now, we've got Winn doing an exhaustive search of sound files from marine biologists, linguists, even cryptozoologists."

Supergirl thought back to when she lived on Krypton. She'd been simply Kara Zor-El then, staying up late to hear her mother, a judge, talk about her job.

One time, Kara's mother had ruled over a case in which the defendant spoke a language nobody on Krypton could translate. Kara had asked her mother how she'd managed to find him innocent.

"Kara," her mother had said, "everyone just wants to be heard. If you're willing to listen, the message will get through—even if you don't understand the words."

Now as Supergirl, Kara stood in front of Prisoner 52, who clearly wanted to be heard. She pressed a hand against the tank and smiled at him.

"We'll find a way to communicate," she promised the creature, as well as Alex and J'onn.

"I sure hope so," said Alex. She took the tablet back from Supergirl and returned it to its holster. "Come on. Tell us more about this crook with spontaneous superpowers," she said, scanning her hand to open the cell door.

"Actually, there were two of them." Supergirl recounted her skirmish with Bee Breather and Lady Levitation as she, J'onn, and Alex walked back to the control room. "I think the woman's powers were new, too. She said she hadn't tried to levitate anything big *yet*."

J'onn nodded. "If she'd had her powers for a while, she'd know what they were capable of."

"Exactly," agreed Supergirl.

"Who are we talking about?" a deep voice spoke up. James Olsen, still in his Guardian armor, came toward the group accompanied by a woman in a police vest.

"Hey, you guys!" Supergirl smiled at them.

Alex approached the woman—her girlfriend, Maggie Sawyer—and gave her a quick peck on the cheek.

"Not that I'm unhappy to see you, but what brings you here?" Alex asked. "It can't be anything good."

"It's not," agreed Maggie. "But I thought the DEO might have intel I don't."

"Is it about normal people suddenly having superpowers?" asked Supergirl.

Maggie's eyebrows lifted. "Yeah, how did you—"

"Ha!" Supergirl pointed at her sister. "See? I knew it!"

Maggie opened her arms wide. "Um . . . *we* still don't." She gestured to herself and James.

"And what we don't know is becoming dangerous," he added, lifting one of his arms to reveal a tear in his suit sleeve.

Winn gasped and leaped out of his chair. "What did you do to my masterpiece?" He rushed over to James, taking the sleeve in hand. In addition to being a mechanical genius, Winn prided himself on being an expert tailor. He'd crafted both Supergirl's and Guardian's costumes.

"*I* didn't do anything. Some old lady in the warehouse district clawed me. And *I'm* fine, thanks for asking," said James, jerking his arm away.

"Sorry. It's just . . ." Winn shoved his hands in his pockets and muttered, "That material's really hard to find."

"So we have another villain out there with spontaneous powers," said Supergirl.

"Actually, she thought I was the villain," James corrected. "Even after I told her I was Guardian!"

"Well, at least we've got one, uh—" J'onn fumbled for the word— "*supercitizen* on our side."

"Supercitizen. Nice." Winn held his fist out to J'onn for a fist bump. J'onn just stared at it.

"I mean, how did that lady not know Guardian?" James continued. "I've been saving lives since way before she jumped in the game."

"Well, a helpful supercitizen isn't necessarily a good thing," said Alex. "Especially if they're taking the law into their own hands."

"Which is why I'm here." Maggie handed her cell phone to Alex. It showed a man's profile on the screen. "Some people saw this man bring down a purse snatcher by shooting poison darts from his fingers."

Winn snorted. "From his fingers? What's he calling himself . . . Digits?"

"He hasn't given himself a name, but that's not bad," mused Maggie.

Supergirl frowned. "I know it's odd to care, but is the purse snatcher OK?"

"He's in critical condition," said Maggie, "and this . . . Digits is still at large."

Alex studied the image for a moment and then looked at Winn. "Can you—"

"Use traffic, ATM, and store cameras to find this guy with facial recognition software?" Winn finished for her. "Just send me the photo."

J'onn put a hand on Supergirl's shoulder. "Winn, see if you can also get security footage from National City Museum and find this Bee Breather and Lady Levitation. I'd hate for them to cross paths with the woman who attacked James."

"Guardian," James corrected.

Winn was already halfway to his computer, a thumbs-up raised above his head.

James turned to Supergirl. "Maybe we should run a piece at CatCo about up-and-coming superheroes."

She smirked at him. "Featuring anyone in particular? As much as I'd love to, I'm not allowed back in the office right now."

James raised an eyebrow. "Says who?"

"I'm gonna guess Snapper Carr," spoke up Alex. She pinched her little sister. "You didn't try to speak his language."

Supergirl threw her hands up. "He wouldn't let me! I have to get this interview with Mayor Lowell, but the mayor doesn't want to talk to anyone from CatCo." She looked at James. "I was hoping you could—"

She was interrupted by a ringtone version of *Newsies'* "Seize the Day" from James's pocket.

"Sorry," he said, taking the phone out. He groaned when he saw the screen and answered the call. "Hey, Snapper." James's eyebrows rose. "Kara? Uh . . . yeah, she's right here." He handed Supergirl the phone, which she took with a mixture of trepidation and confusion.

"Hey, Chief! How'd you know I'd be with James?" she asked.

"I'm an investigative reporter," Snapper said in a bored voice. "Tracking people down is half my job. Listen, everyone else is on assignment, and since I assume you've gotten nowhere with *yours*," he said pointedly, "I need you to interview someone at Eighth and Palmer."

Supergirl blinked rapidly but didn't say anything until James nudged her. "Uh . . . yes! Of course, Chief." She reached for a notepad and pen. "Who's at Eighth and Palmer?"

Snapper sighed. "I was afraid you were going to ask. There's a structure fire, and a woman—Jacqueline Reyes— is supposedly putting it out with rain clouds she created in her bare hands."

"She can create rain clouds with her bare hands?" Supergirl repeated loudly enough for her friends to hear.

"I know, it sounds ridiculous," Snapper said, misreading her tone, "but it seems Supergirl isn't the only superhero in National City anymore."

"I'm on it." Supergirl hung up and handed the phone back to James.

"What's this woman's name?" asked Winn, fingers poised over his keyboard.

"Jacqueline Reyes," Supergirl supplied. "And if you'll all excuse me, I have a city to . . . watch someone else save." She cocked her head to one side. "Weird."

Supergirl zipped back to the museum to grab the clothes she'd left on the roof and then landed in an alley near the fire to change into Kara Danvers. She couldn't risk being seen flying around in her work clothes, and she couldn't appear as Supergirl because then she'd be expected to help put out the fire. All focus would be off Jacqueline Reyes, and Kara would lose the interview.

Luckily, Kara's powers gave her a speed boost, and she walked several blocks in a minute before a traffic light stopped her. While she waited for it to change, Kara searched social media for Jacqueline Reyes. There were several in the city, but none were known superheroes. She thought about the old lady who attacked James. It was pretty unlikely *she* was a superhero, either.

That made five supercitizens. In one day.

*It can't be a coincidence*, she thought. *How are they all tied together?*

The light turned green and Kara stepped off the curb, switching screens on her phone so she could text Alex. A second later, tires screeched and a horn blared in Kara's ear. She turned to stare, wide-eyed, at the front grille of a delivery truck.

On instinct, Kara crouched and braced herself, holding out both hands to stop the truck. It might give away her identity, but it was better than being roadkill.

Before she even touched metal, however, another pair of hands—male, by the looks of them—reached the truck before hers could. The hood crumpled, and the truck's tires shivered as it skidded to a stop.

Kara let out a deep breath. "Perfect timing."

She put a hand on Mon-El's and went to kiss him. Then she froze.

The guy who'd stopped the truck wasn't Mon-El.

It was Marcus, the guy who worked the coffee bar at Noonan's.

# 4

MARCUS HAD HIS EYES CLOSED and his lips puckered, ready to receive Kara's kiss. She leaned away. "You have superpowers?"

Marcus opened his eyes and grinned at her. "Pretty cool, right?" He squinted at Kara and snapped his fingers. "Wait a minute, I know you! Carka!"

Kara didn't bother to correct him. "When did you get superpowers? *How* did you get them?"

Police sirens wailed nearby, and Marcus cringed.

"Listen, I'm new to this superhero thing, but I'm pretty sure I'm not supposed to be here when the cops show up. Gotta bolt." Marcus started to run, but Kara chased after him.

"Wait!" she said, grabbing his arm.

Marcus spun around, all smiles. "OK, if it means that

much to you." Before Kara could react, he grabbed her waist and pulled her close, smashing his lips against hers.

He tasted like coffee and cluelessness.

She pushed away from him, and he dashed off with a wink.

"Don't expect to see me at Noonan's anymore. I'm a hero now!" he cried, bending his knees and leaping forward awkwardly. "Nope, can't fly yet."

Kara snickered and watched him go. Then a passing fire truck reminded her of what she was supposed to be doing in the first place.

"Shoot! Jacqueline Reyes!"

Kara supersprinted the rest of the way to Eighth and Palmer, where a crowd had formed outside the building's smoldering remains. A crowd that included several news vans.

She definitely wasn't getting the first interview with this woman.

Kara pushed her way through the throng of people toward the news reporters and camera operators. At least a dozen microphones were pointed at the face of a pretty Latina woman wearing a dress and heels. She flashed each camera a gleaming smile as she spoke to the press, all poise and confidence.

"I couldn't very well wait for the weather to change. We're

not expecting rain until the weekend." Jacqueline Reyes winked at the crowd. "I should know."

Everyone except Kara laughed.

"So I decided to put the fire out myself," concluded Jacqueline. "It's a handy little gift, controlling the weather." She held out one hand, palm up, and wriggled the fingers of her other hand above it. A tiny dark cloud formed in the space between her hands, and soon a flurry of small white flakes fell from it.

The crowd erupted in applause and excited chatter, and the reporters shouted more questions.

"Is this why your weather reports are always so accurate?"

"Do you have other powers?"

"Are you working with Supergirl?"

Kara's eyebrows went up at the first question, and she half listened to the answers as she pulled up a web browser on her phone. A search for "Jacqueline Reyes meteorologist" revealed a publicity photo of the woman standing in front of her.

Jacqueline Reyes reported the weather and could control it, Kara thought, which might have meant a person's job determined their power—if it weren't for Marcus. He was superstrong, but that had nothing to do with taking coffee orders.

"I expect Supergirl and I will team up soon," Jaqueline responded.

Kara shook her head. Jacqueline was drawing way too

much attention to herself. Hinting that she might know Supergirl could endanger her life, especially if these powers weren't permanent.

It was time to clear the crowd.

"You're pretty confident for someone who just got her superpower today!" shouted Kara.

Jacqueline's confident smile faltered. Half the reporters turned toward Kara, and the other half kept their microphones trained on the meteorologist.

"I'm not sure what you mean," said Jacqueline. She blinked rapidly and brought back her smile. "I've always had this power."

"Really? Because there are supercitizens popping up all over the city today," said Kara.

Now all the microphones and cameras were on her.

"There are?" someone asked.

"Where?" another reporter chimed in.

"The police are after a guy with poison darts for fingernails, there's an old lady with claws in the warehouse district, and an employee at Noonan's has superstrength," Kara told them.

She left out the fact that Marcus wouldn't be there anymore.

The reporters spoke or motioned to their camera crews, and soon most of the media were on the road, leaving Kara to confront a glowering Jacqueline.

"Who do you think you are?" asked Jacqueline, glaring at Kara.

"Someone who doesn't want to see you get killed," said Kara. "We need to talk."

Alex hated charades.

When she and her friends played on game nights, nobody could understand what she was acting out, and Kara would eventually have to use her X-ray vison to read the answer on the card.

But charades was all Alex could think to do as she and Prisoner 52 stared at each other through the side of the tank at the DEO.

"Why are you here?" Alex shrugged her shoulders, pointed to Prisoner 52, then pointed to the ground. She hoped body language was universal. For all she knew, she'd just told the creature that his mother was a sea horse.

In response to her gestures, Prisoner 52 screeched and squawked.

Alex sighed. "Yeah, you and me both, buddy."

The cell door slid open, and J'onn and Winn joined her.

"How's Bubbles?" asked Winn.

"Bubbles?" Alex repeated with a smirk.

"Prisoner 52," J'onn said, frowning at Winn.

"See, to me, that feels a little impersonal," said Winn.

"All the other inmates have names." He stopped and corrected himself. "Except the one who uses a symbol. Like Prince."

"Well, Bubbles is doing fine," said Alex, smiling at the way the name made J'onn's forehead crinkle. "But I still can't tell you a thing about him or why he's here."

Winn held up a finger. "I thought you might say that. I came up with something that should help."

He reached into a bag he'd brought and pulled out what looked like a cycling helmet with several wires running off it. Each wire ended with an electrode disk, except for one that had a 3.5 mm connector.

"You're going to try an EEG?" asked Alex.

An electroencephalograph was good for monitoring electrical activity in the brain, but Alex didn't think Bubbles had any problems with his mental faculties.

"It's sort of an EEG," said Winn, turning the helmet over in one hand. "Except this device won't just chart Bubbles's brain activity. It'll let us *see* what he's thinking. I call it the camera cogitari."

Alex glanced at Bubbles, who was watching their conversation with rapt attention. "And how are you planning to get him to wear it?"

"He doesn't have to," said J'onn, taking the helmet from Winn. "I'll read his mind—"

"And what was his name again?" interrupted Winn, blinking innocently.

J'onn grunted. "I'll read *the creature's* mind and make his thoughts my own." He put on the helmet. "Because, trust me, you don't want to see what *I'm* thinking right now."

Alex hid a smile while Winn attached the electrodes to J'onn's scalp. Then Winn took the tablet computer from its wall holster and plugged in the helmet's connecting wire. He tapped the tablet screen a few times and nodded to J'onn.

"Whenever you're ready," Winn said.

He and J'onn approached Bubbles's tank, and J'onn closed his eyes, breathing deeply. Alex watched over Winn's shoulder as images from J'onn's mind—or, rather, Bubbles's mind—appeared on the screen.

"Wow," whispered Alex.

It would be wrong to call what she saw an ordinary city. This was a haunting masterpiece. Around a central tower stood stone buildings trimmed in gold and supported by pillars with even more gold-inlaid images and writing. Scattered about the city were statues of unfamiliar figures and bridges that joined crumbling roadways. Every structure held a greenish hue and fluttered with the activity of tropical fish darting about.

Because the entire city was underwater.

Suddenly, the image of the city was replaced by two

scuba divers in black wet suits. They were swimming from the city toward the surface with a length of netting between them, something nestled in its midst.

Another image replaced that one: a man slipping into the tank at the National City Aquarium's deep-sea exhibit . . . while wearing a black wet suit.

"That's why Bubbles attacked the aquarium employee," said Alex, pointing at the screen.

Winn nodded. "He thought it was one of the guys who took something from his city."

The image on the screen turned black as J'onn opened his eyes and removed the helmet.

"Any idea where this city is?" he asked.

Winn shrugged. "There are all kinds of sunken places in the world: Port Royal in Jamaica, Cleopatra's palace in Egypt . . ." He cleared his throat, and in a softer voice added, "Atlantis."

"Atlantis?" Alex said skeptically, crossing her arms. "The mythical city of demigods that nobody's ever been able to find?"

Winn mirrored her stance. "We work for a department that monitors aliens, your sister can fly, and we know a speedster from an alternate Earth. Not to mention we've got a giant sea monkey in a tank." He gestured to Bubbles. "But Atlantis seems unbelievable?"

"He has a point," said J'onn before Alex could argue.

"Winn, did you save those images when you extracted them from my mind?"

"Of course," said Winn. "And I thought I'd do a reverse photo lookup for matches."

J'onn nodded approvingly. "Get on it."

As Winn was putting the helmet and tablet away, Alex's phone rang with a call from Kara.

"Hey, you! How's the interview going?" she asked, putting her sister on speaker.

"It's not, actually," said Kara. "I just got done scolding Jacqueline Reyes about showing off her powers. What have you learned about her? All I know is she's a meteorologist."

Winn bit his lip. "I was working on a project for J'onn. But I can look her up now."

He grabbed his bag and hurried from Bubbles's holding cell, with Alex and J'onn following.

"While we're at it, what did you find out about the robbers from the museum?" Kara asked as Winn, Alex, and J'onn entered the control room.

"Is that Kara on the phone?" Mon-El asked, swiveling in Winn's chair. "Tell her I took care of the mess at the museum, but Supergirl's going to have to make an appearance at their annual fund-raiser."

"Thanks, babe!" said Kara.

"Move, babe." Winn shooed Mon-El away and took his place, feet dangling above the floor. "Holy crap, you're tall." He adjusted the chair and clacked away on his keyboard. "I got some results when I cross-referenced museum surveillance images through our facial recognition software. Looks like Bee Breather's real name is Wendell Geary. He works at an auto shop and—get this—keeps bees on the roof of his apartment as a hobby."

"Interesting," said Kara. "And Lady Levitation?"

"That's Samantha Coen," said Alex. "She works at the auto shop with Wendell, and she's an amateur bodybuilder on the side."

Mon-El's eyes widened. "She builds bodies? Out of what, car parts? No wonder she's an amateur."

"She builds up her own body," explained J'onn, making a muscle. "Strength training."

"Oh." Mon-El relaxed and laughed. "You mean she lifts weights." He rubbed his chin. "I wonder if that's why her superpower is levitation."

"It would make sense," said J'onn. "She's interested in lifting things, Bee Breather was interested in bees, and the meteorologist is obviously interested in the weather."

"You guys might be right," said Kara. "But it still doesn't explain why the counter guy at Noonan's has superstrength."

"Wait, what?" Alex gave her phone a perplexed look. "The one who was flirting with you this morning?"

"Flirting with who now?" Mon-El stepped closer to the phone.

Alex shushed him with a look. "He has superstrength?"

"He saved me from getting hit by a truck, Alex," said Kara. "But I couldn't get him to tell me how he got his powers. He just kissed me and ran off."

"He"—Mon-El grabbed the phone from Alex—"he kissed you? Like, on the face?"

Kara chuckled. "It was my fault. When Marcus saved me, I thought it was you at first, so I went to kiss him. I backed away when I realized it wasn't."

"Aw." Mon-El ducked his head and grinned. "You thought it was me?" His expression sobered. "Wait. After you backed away, he still kissed you?" Mon-El thrust the phone at Alex and walked over to Winn's chair. "What's this Marcus guy's last name and where does he live?"

"Mon-El . . ." Kara's tone of warning carried through the phone.

"According to the Noonan's employee database, his last name is Gaius, and he lives in Shady Oaks apartments," said Winn. Then he frowned, his eyes caught by something else on his screen. "Hold up. So does Jacqueline Reyes."

Winn transfered the data to the video wall.

"Could their powers have literally come from the same place?" Alex asked J'onn.

"It's possible. Winn, where do Wendell Geary and Samantha Coen live?" asked J'onn.

With a few more mouse clicks, Winn said, "Wendell Geary's also at Shady Oaks, but not Samantha Coen." He tapped a few keys. "And that guy Digits lives there too!"

"Four out of five is too big to be a coincidence," said Alex.

"Lady and gentlemen, we've got an origin point!" Kara cheered through the phone. "I wish I could check it out right now, but I have to get yelled at by Snapper."

J'onn and Alex exchanged a look.

"Someone should stay with Bubbles," said Alex.

Mon-El raised a hand. "You can both stay, and I can check out the apartment complex."

J'onn frowned. "You shouldn't go alone. If whatever happened affected everyone in the building, they could all have superpowers."

Mon-El nodded and glanced at Winn. "Text James. We may need Guardian."

# 5

**K**ARA HAD HOPED TO RETURN TO CatCo victorious, with the Jacqueline Reyes interview in hand. After she'd warned the storm bringer about using her power, however, the woman had turned out to be even colder than the snow she could muster.

"What you did for this city was wonderful, but you're not Supergirl," Kara had told her. "You're human and fragile. Supergirl's an alien who can withstand bullets and being tossed across the room, either of which could kill you."

Jacqueline had curled her lip and twirled one finger. A strong wind whipped around Kara, who shielded her eyes to avoid the ashes and embers from the smoldering building nearby.

"Sweetheart, with one motion, I can whisk bullets aside

or cushion my landing," Jacqueline said, clenching her fist to stifle the wind. "I don't need to be an alien. And you don't need to be jealous. Now, if you'll excuse me, I've got a city to save."

Jacqueline walked away and hailed a cab.

"I'm not jealous!" Kara shouted after her. "I'm worried about your life!"

Now Kara was on her way up the CatCo elevator, worried about her own life. Or at least her future at CatCo. She hadn't gotten the interview with the mayor, and she hadn't gotten the interview with Jacqueline Reyes. In that moment, calling herself a reporter felt like a bit of a stretch. She had a feeling Snapper would think the same.

When she saw Snapper's desk empty, Kara's heart gave a hopeful leap. But it just as quickly plummeted when she realized he was standing in the media room, watching the local news stations. Jacqueline Reyes appeared on all of them: News 25, News 37, Channel 68—each station featuring slightly different sound bites and chyron, captioning details about the meteorologist across the bottom of the screen.

"Great," Kara muttered.

She adjusted her glasses and skulked toward Snapper, hands clasped in front of her.

"I know what it looks like," she started.

"I know what it *doesn't* look like," he responded, not taking his eyes off the screens. "The exclusive you told me you'd get. Did you let this one cancel the interview, too?" He gestured at Jacqueline's image.

Kara winced and hurried forward. "The interview wasn't worth pursuing, Chief. Trust me. By tomorrow, she'll be old news."

Snapper finally turned to face Kara, scowling. "Of course she'll be old news tomorrow. That's how news works, Ponytail. And it's why we want to get it *first*." He brushed past Kara to return to his desk.

"She's not the only supercitizen I've come across today," Kara informed him. "And I'm pretty sure she won't be the last."

"*Supercitizen*?" Snapper spat the word out as if it tasted bad. "What kind of millennial garbage is that?"

Kara fought back a smile. If only he knew it came from the mouth of a centuries-old Martian.

"There's a bigger story here. Not just Jacqueline Reyes," said Kara. "Where are these supercitizens getting their powers? What does it mean for the future of National City?"

Snapper chewed on his pen and didn't interrupt her, so Kara kept going. At first, she'd brought up the supercitizens to convince him to forget Jacqueline Reyes. But now she felt a potential story brewing.

"These supercitizens all have something in common. I traced them back to one location."

Snapper took the pen out of his mouth. "How?"

Kara cleared her throat and fidgeted with her glasses.

Snapper sighed. "Danvers, if you say Supergirl—"

"An anonymous source," Kara said instead.

"Oh, that's much better," he muttered, dropping his pen.

Kara paced in front of his desk. "Sir, Jacqueline Reyes wasn't a story, but I think this . . . this surge of supercitizens could be."

"This *surge* is already all over the news!" Snapper gestured to the media room. "Provided by one of my own reporters, who should have kept the info to herself." He arched an eyebrow at Kara.

That had definitely come back to bite her.

Kara took a deep breath. "The surge might be on the news, but not the details. I can get those."

Snapper grunted and massaged his eyes. "Fine, you can work this 'supercitizen' story." He stressed the word with air quotes. "But I still want that interview with the mayor."

It was all Kara could do to keep from flopping onto the floor and throwing a tantrum.

"But Mayor Lowell doesn't want to talk to anyone at CatCo!" she said in exasperation. "Do you have any idea why?"

"Maybe he went on a bad date with Cat Grant," her boss suggested. "Although I guess *bad* date's a little redundant when it comes to Cat." He smirked.

"Hey, Ms. Grant is a wonderful person!" said Kara.

Snapper didn't look swayed. "You know she can't hear you, right?"

"Mayor Lowell was fine with the interview until last week," Kara continued. "So something we published recently must have changed his mind."

Snapper reached into a pile of papers on his desk and yanked out a copy of the latest *CatCo* magazine. "You want answers? Knock yourself out."

He handed the magazine to Kara. "I want that super-citizen story and an interview with the mayor lined up by Wednesday." He stopped a man walking past and handed him a paper marked in red ink. "Too many words. Too little substance."

Kara's mouth dropped open. "This Wednesday? As in two days from now?"

Snapper blinked at her. "You can turn it in sooner if you want."

Without another word, Kara pressed the magazine to her chest and retreated to an empty nook to flip through the pages.

None of the letters to the editor mentioned the mayor,

nor did the section on fashion don'ts, current events, or any of the featured articles. Mayor Lowell didn't have a wife or kids, so there was no offense to be had there. If he was upset at CatCo, it wasn't because of the latest issue of the magazine.

Which meant it had to be an earlier one.

Kara sighed and headed for the archives.

*I hope Mon-El and James are having better luck with* their *investigation*, she thought.

Mon-El and James were sitting in a car across from Shady Oaks apartments, waiting for someone, *anyone*, to step outside. Mon-El had already tried calling random tenants over the speaker box, but nobody wanted to let him in.

"This town makes people too suspicious," he muttered, slurping on a shake from Noonan's.

"Yeah, it's the town. Not you," said James with a chuckle.

Mon-El gave him a withering look. "What makes *me* seem suspicious?"

"Gee, I don't know. Maybe the reasons you want into the building. They sound incredibly made up."

Mon-El threw his hands in the air. "Flower delivery is a real thing."

"Yes." James leaned toward him. "But not when the flowers come from 'Um . . . Er . . . That Place by the Dry Cleaner.' "

Mon-El made a face. "Yeah, that may not have been my strongest lie."

James pointed past him. "Here we go. Old lady taking her dog for a walk."

They both got out of the car, and James smoothed his shirt.

"Excuse me, ma'am?" He trotted up to the woman and her German shepherd; the latter growled low in her throat.

"It's all right, Precious." The woman patted her dog on the head while smiling up at James. "What can I do for you, son?"

"I'm James Olsen, and this is Mike Matthews." He gestured to Mon-El. "We're with the *Tribune* and wanted to interview someone who lives in the building. Have you seen anything . . . strange going on today?"

The woman frowned. "What do you mean?"

Mon-El watched her reach for Precious, fingers touching empty space a few times before they connected with fur.

"Uh . . . James?" he mumbled.

"Have you seen anyone who looks unusual?" James tried again. "Maybe a woman with really long fingernails or a guy surrounded by a bunch of bees?"

The woman looked at James . . . slightly past him, actually.

"I'm sorry," the woman said. "I haven't seen anything like that."

*Of course she hasn't,* Mon-El thought. *Because she's blind.*

"Ja-ames," Mon-El singsonged.

James smiled at the woman. "Excuse us for a second." He pulled Mon-El aside. "What, man?"

Mon-El pointed at his eyes with one finger and at the old woman with another, shaking his head. "I don't think she wants to tell us she's blind," Mon-El said in a low voice. "This looks like the type of neighborhood where someone could take advantage of that."

James nodded and patted him on the shoulder. "Good call."

They rejoined the old woman, and James picked up where he left off.

"So you didn't see anything. But did you hear anything?" he asked her.

The woman's smile broadened. "I'm afraid I have fairly quiet neighbors. They don't like to disturb me, you see, since I own the building."

Mon-El stepped closer to the old woman and lowered his voice. "If you own the building, then you should be concerned about the safety of everyone inside. Are you sure you didn't come across anything suspicious today?"

Precious whined and pawed at the old woman's leg, and she nodded. "Well, now that you mention it, a tenant on the fifth floor had a little accident."

"An accident?" James repeated.

She nodded again. "There was this loud boom that rattled the windows. Dr. Wanabi said his blender exploded when he was making a smoothie, but I've had my doubts."

Mon-El and James looked at each another.

"Can we see if Dr. Wanabi's home?" asked James.

The woman frowned. "I don't know . . ."

"We just want to ask a few questions."

"And we can check on the place for you," said Mon-El.

The old woman grew quiet for a moment and then nodded. "All right. But I'm coming with you." She tugged on Precious's leash. "Let's go home."

The lobby of the building was small but inviting with a few well-worn chairs and a table holding a pod coffee machine and foam cups.

"How many people live here?" Mon-El asked, peeking down a corridor. There were welcome mats in front of a few doors, but nothing out of the ordinary.

The old woman pushed the up button for the elevator. "More than a hundred."

Mon-El glanced back at James. A hundred potential supercitizens.

The elevator dinged, and the door slid open.

"Dr. Wanabi's on the top floor," she reminded them, stepping in with Precious, "Apartment 500."

Mon-El and James joined them, and James pressed the button. A short ride later, the elevator dinged again, and the door opened onto the fifth floor.

And absolute darkness.

Mon-El squinted into the black and saw nothing. But he heard at least a dozen unnatural sounds.

Precious whined and pressed against the old woman, who stroked the dog's head.

"Maybe Precious and I should let you boys visit Dr. Wanabi on your own," she told James and Mon-El.

"Down the hall to your right," she said.

Mon-El took his phone from his pocket and turned on its flashlight. "Wait for us downstairs," he told the old woman. "If we're not there in ten minutes, call 911."

He and James stepped into the hallway, which grew even darker as the elevator doors closed.

"What do you think this is?" asked James, lighting up his own phone.

"I think someone doesn't want to be seen," said Mon-El. "And not because they're throwing a surprise party."

They crept down the hallway, Mon-El dropping into a stooped walk, his muscles coiled for whatever came next.

James shone a light on the closest apartment door.

"Number 508. We have a ways to go," he said.

Mon-El nodded. "If it's anything like the horror movies

I've seen, Dr. Wanabi's apartment will be at the end of the corridor, across from a portal to hell. Also, our flashlights will stop working right before we get there."

James swallowed audibly. "I see you've got jokes."

"Yeah, the funny guy lives the longest."

Wispy vapor curled out from under the closed door of number 508 .

"The guy who stays to see what *that* is does not." Mon-El clasped James's shoulder and pushed him down the corridor toward number 500.

Each apartment they passed confirmed that something strange had definitely happened in the building. The door of number 507 had deep grooves in its surface. The door of number 506 bore a sloppy sign with INVISIBLE BUT HOME written on it. Number 505 didn't have a door, but a pair of glowing eyes watched Mon-El and James as they passed. The only door that seemed fairly normal was number 500.

"How do we want to do this?" asked Mon-El, cracking his knuckles. "Pick the lock? Bust it down?"

James pressed the doorbell.

"Also effective," said Mon-El.

As the door opened, daylight obliterated the darkness, causing both Mon-El and James to squint and blink.

"Finally!" A stocky Japanese man in black rubber gloves and safety apron came into view. "What took—" At the sight of Mon-El and James, his eyes widened. "Oh, sorry. What can I do for you?"

"Dr. Wanabi?" said James, raising his hands to show he was harmless. "We were hoping you could help us with a problem."

Dr. Wanabi smiled. "Of course. Please come in." He opened the door wide. "I'm so sorry for your troubles. What floor?" Dr. Wanabi indicated a couch.

"Floor?" James repeated, perching on the edge of a couch cushion.

"Do you live on?" asked Dr. Wanabi. He picked up a notebook from his coffee table. "I'm curious how far the effects went."

James's forehead wrinkled and his lips formed another question.

"Third!" blurted Mon-El. "We live on the third floor of this building."

Understanding showed in James's eyes.

"Yeah . . . yes. That's right."

Dr. Wanabi nodded. "That's a relief. It doesn't appear to have spread any lower than the third floor." He jotted a note. "And what are your names and superpowers?"

"Uh, well, I'm James." James looked to Mon-El. "But Mike's power is more impressive than mine."

*Which doesn't exist*, Mon-El silently added.

Out loud, he said, "I'm Mike, and I have superstrength." He pounded a fist on the coffee table, breaking it in half.

Dr. Wanabi looked down at the remains of his table and frowned. "You don't have to use your power. You just have to tell me about it."

"Sorry." Mon-El winced and tried to reassemble the broken furniture.

"And what about you, James?" Dr. Wanabi asked as he wrote.

"Me?" James repeated with a nervous chuckle. "My power?" He glanced around the room, his gaze stopping on a vase of flowers. "I can make plants grow."

Dr. Wanabi looked up from his notebook. "Really? I have a tomato plant on my balcony that could use some help."

"Oh!" James scratched his head. "I thought you, uh, didn't want us to use our powers."

"Yeah, and James's is uncontrollable," said Mon-El, making a face. "He might save your tomato plant or turn it into an eight-foot, man-eating—"

"Mon-El!" James said, giving him a look.

"Mon-El?" Dr. Wanabi shook his head. "I thought you were Mike. What's going on?"

"Nothing!" said Mon-El. "We just wanted to know more about our powers. You know, where they came from, how long they'll last, that sort of thing."

"That information was on the flyers I put under everyone's doors." Dr. Wanabi took a step back. "You're not tenants, are you?"

Mon-El grabbed his arm. "Listen, Dr. Wanabi, we can explain."

For the second time, Dr. Wanabi's eyes widened. For the first time, Mon-El found himself looking directly into them instead of down at them.

"What—" he began, but his question was drowned in the doctor's screams.

Instantly, Mon-El released him. "Hey, I'm sorry." He held up his hands in submission—hands that were now wearing black gloves, connecting to arms that weren't his own. "Whoa!" Mon-El turned toward James, who was gaping at him, slack-jawed.

"You're . . . you're . . ."

Mon-El darted for the nearest reflective surface: a china cabinet door. Instead of his own face, Mon-El saw Dr. Wanabi's.

"I look like you!" he turned and exclaimed to the doctor.

But the doctor wasn't there.

"Where did Dr. Wanabi go?" asked Mon-El.

James glanced around. "He's not here."

Mon-El stared at him. "Thanks. I figured that out."

"No, I mean he's not in any of these rooms." James stared at the living room wall with an awestruck expression.

"How can you tell?" Mon-El asked as his friend ventured further into the apartment. "Hey! Where are you going?"

"He's headed for the balcony!" James called. "I saw him through the wall."

"You what?" Mon-El gave chase and almost collided with James in the balcony doorway.

They both watched as Dr. Wanabi was carried away by a woman wearing something that looked like a drone propeller on her back.

"This is a really weird day," said Mon-El.

"Yep," said James, closing the balcony door. "Let's see if we can figure out what started it all."

# 6

**N**OTHING.

Kara had found nothing in the archives that might have offended Mayor Lowell. As far as she could tell, *CatCo* magazine's only fault was telling people that shirts with buckles would be the next big thing. All the models looked as if they were wearing Arkham Asylum straitjackets.

She looked at the bank of wall clocks showing times around the world. In National City, it was well past time to go home for the day.

Kara sighed and stretched. Gathering the stack of magazines she'd pulled, she returned them to the archives. On her way out of the office, she waved at a coworker who was running to the media room near Snapper's desk. Then another reporter rushed past Kara. And another. All headed to the media room.

"This can't be good," she muttered, following them.

". . . avoid all streets near Riverdale and Maple," a news anchor on one of the stations was saying. "These lions are *not* domesticated."

"What's happening?" asked Kara. She turned her attention to a different station that had an image of the National City Zoo and a chyron across the bottom: *2 lions, 3 tigers escape from cages.* "Lions and tigers?"

"But no bears," someone added. "Oh my."

Everyone laughed except Kara.

Because she was already headed for the roof, changing into Supergirl.

"Kara?" Winn spoke in her ear over comms. "I know you're at work, but there's a situation—"

"At Riverdale and Maple?" she asked, stepping outside. "The loose lions?"

"Uh, yeah! And I don't think you can distract these cats with a ball of string—unless it's *really* big," said Winn.

"I'm on it." Supergirl cocked her head and listened.

Roars and screams were intermingled with the sounds of a woman's shouting voice.

"Sit! SIT!"

Supergirl launched herself from the rooftop and zipped

across town to the source of the commotion. People and cars were fleeing en masse from a lion and lioness prowling in front of a movie theater. The only person not running was a young woman in a hijab who was waving her arms at the lion and lioness.

Supergirl swooped down beside the young woman. "You should leave, miss. This could turn dangerous."

The young woman regarded her with wide eyes. "Supergirl!" She pressed a hand to her chest. "I am such a huge fan."

Supergirl smiled tightly. "Thanks. Now, you'd better let me handle these wild animals."

The young woman shook her head. "I freed them. I need to fix this."

It was Supergirl's turn to be awestruck. "You're the one who released these animals from the zoo?"

The young woman nodded and wrung her hands together. "I was able to control my cat at home, so I wanted to try on something bigger."

Supergirl groaned. "You couldn't do that while they were still in cages?" Nearby, the lion roared, and Supergirl felt the vibration in her chest. "It doesn't matter. What's your name?"

"Reshma," said the young woman.

"OK, Reshma, you have to go so I can do my job."

Reshma fixed pleading eyes on Supergirl. "But I can make things better!"

Supergirl gave Reshma an apologetic smile. "This isn't up for debate."

She grabbed the young woman around the waist and flew her several blocks away to a cat café.

"Get one of these critters to make you a cappuccino, and then we'll talk," said Supergirl.

She took off again, her mind moving even faster than she was.

How was she going to capture these big cats?

If they'd been criminals, she would've knocked them out with a good right hook, but somehow punching a cat seemed wrong, no matter what size it was. Using her freeze breath and heat vision on them were out of the question, too. She just needed to contain them until the zoo officials could take them back. But National City didn't exactly have lion-sized cat carriers.

Or did it?

Supergirl headed for the shipyard and found exactly what she was looking for: steel shipping containers. She dug her hands into the side of an empty one and squeezed until the metal conformed under her fingers. Then, with a grunt, she hoisted it above her head and lifted it in the sky.

Thankfully, the lion and his mate had chosen to make the

movie theater their new habitat, and Supergirl didn't see any evidence that they'd nibbled on a pedestrian while she was away.

She lowered the shipping container into an alley beside the movie theater and opened one of the doors.

"Sorry about this," she told the lion and lioness as she flew above them.

They watched curiously—and then yowled, springing to their feet as the asphalt around them became riddled with searing hot divots from Supergirl's heat vision. She herded the lion and lioness into the alley and the safety of the shipping container, closing the door behind them. She considered flying the container back to the zoo, but there were still tigers on the loose.

Supergirl tore air holes into the top of the shipping container and caught the attention of a police officer who was cordoning off the area. "Don't let anyone open this container unless they're with the zoo!"

He nodded, and Supergirl went in search of the tigers. The news reports had mentioned there were three, so she hoped they liked to be together.

"If I were a tiger, where would I go?" she wondered aloud. It wouldn't do to listen for them, since they didn't roar as much as lions. She thought back to a field trip to the zoo she'd taken in junior high. The tigers there had splashed around in a giant pool. "The natural springs!"

The sun was setting, but Supergirl picked out the three tigers swimming and diving. It would be tough to corral them by hand, but she could always force them from the water a different way.

Supergirl approached the spring's shore, riddled with hastily abandoned beach towels and drink coolers. She puckered her lips and blew on the water, her freeze breath chilling the natural springs until ice began to form on the shoreline.

"That should do it," she said. And sure enough, a moment later, all three tigers swam for shore.

She was about to steer them into a nearby public restroom when she heard footsteps approach from behind. The tigers heard them, too, and three pairs of ears perked up as the beasts paused and sniffed the air.

"Stay back!" Supergirl shouted to a man in coveralls. "There are tigers nearby."

"I know," he said with a chuckle. "I'm here to help you, Supergirl."

One of the smaller tigers trundled toward Supergirl and the man in coveralls.

Supergirl placed herself between them. "Are you a tiger tamer?" she asked him.

"No, but I can do *this*." The man squatted and touched his palms to the grass. The earth began to shake and rumble as it separated beneath his hands.

Supergirl leaped into the air and watched as the fissure widened and deepened. It curved around the tigers until they stood on a small plot of grass surrounded by a yawning chasm too wide for them to jump.

The tigers sniffed the edges of their dirt island but made no motion to leave it.

"Ta-da!" said the man, holding his arms open.

Supergirl was about to compliment him when the earth shook for a second time and a geyser of water shot into the sky.

She closed her eyes and fought the urge to scream as droplets rained down. "When you moved the earth, did you check for water lines?" she asked the man in coveralls.

He sucked in his breath and let out a nervous chuckle. "Whoops."

These supercitizens had no idea what they were doing. The first thing Supergirl *always* did was think of what consequences her actions might have.

Supergirl pointed toward the street. "Go."

"Sorry about this," he said, backing away. "It's my first day as a superhero."

She forced a smile. "Just *go!*"

The man sprinted away, and Supergirl dove into the fissure to find the busted pipe. A quick blast from her heat vision sealed it, but even in those few minutes, dirt had made its way into the water supply.

"Winn?" Supergirl spoke into the growing darkness.

"What's going on, Catwoman?" She heard him chuckle to himself.

"I need you to contact the water plant," she said. "I had to repair a busted pipe out by the natural springs. Nobody should drink the water."

On the other end of the line, Winn made a sputtering, spitting sound. "Thanks for the warning *after* I drink from the fountain. How goes the kitty corralling?"

"I'm all done. The zoo just needs to pick them up."

"Great! I'll start making some calls. In the mean-time, Alex and J'onn want you at the DEO," said Winn. "James and Mon-El are back from Shady Oaks, new and improved."

Supergirl frowned, unsure what that meant. "Give me a few minutes," she said. "There's something I have to take care of first."

"See you on the flip side."

Supergirl flew to the CatCo building and landed on the balcony of the twentieth floor. These supercitizens were getting out of control. They had no clue how to use their powers and were as much a danger to themselves as they were to everyone around them. It needed to stop.

Still dressed as Supergirl, she strode up to Snapper's desk, standing before him with her hands on her hips.

Snapper barely glanced up from the news article he was editing. "Your superhero pose stinks. Or you do. Either way, step back from my desk."

"I need to get a video message to the people of National City, and I need to do it *now*," said Supergirl.

Her urgent tone did nothing to sway Snapper. "Post something on YouTube," he said. "And make sure you include a cat. People won't care unless it has a cat." He snapped his fingers and wrinkled his nose. "*That's* what that smell is."

"I can't wait for it to go viral." She paused and added, "This will be great exposure for CatCo! A Supergirl exclusive."

Snapper snorted. "Yeah, because CatCo's really hurting for attention." He grabbed his coffee mug and got out of his chair.

"Please." Supergirl stepped into his path. "There are supercitizens all over National City putting themselves and others in danger. I can't do this without you."

Snapper regarded her for a moment. "I don't work with the news crew," he finally said. "But I know they wouldn't say no to you. Be on the tenth floor in three minutes," he continued. "I'll let them know you're coming."

"Thank you!" Supergirl reached out to touch his arm but pulled back at the stern look on Snapper's face. "Sorry."

"Don't apologize to me," he said. "Apologize to my reporter whose exclusive you just stole."

Snapper sat back down and picked up his phone. Supergirl hurried to the balcony, silently swearing. The reporter he was referring to was her alter ego, Kara. And he was right. She'd just stolen the exclusive from herself!

Supergirl counted balconies as she passed them, stopping on the one for the tenth floor. A young guy with headphones around his neck was waiting for her.

"It's really you!" He gawked as she landed lightly in front of him.

"I'm sorry this is so sudden," she said with a wave. "Could I borrow your camera crew for a couple minutes?"

"Of course!" He motioned for her to follow. "The studio's this way."

They entered an enormous room bedecked with dozens of lights on the ceiling, a green screen behind a news desk, and four different cameras aimed at the news anchors.

When they saw Supergirl, both news anchors stood, and the camera crew applauded.

Supergirl grinned and waved away their appreciation. "Thank you for letting me come. I'm sorry if I'm interrupting an important broadcast."

She approached the news desk and shook hands with the anchors and the news director.

"We were just about to cover some interesting stories from today, including one where you stepped in and captured some zoo cats." The female news anchor pointed at Supergirl.

"Actually, that's why I was hoping to be on your show," said Supergirl. "The supercitizens are getting out of control."

The news anchors looked at each other.

"Out of control?" the male anchor repeated.

It pained Supergirl to give up the information, but at least the exclusive would stay within CatCo. And it was still technically her story; she was just telling it while wearing a flame-retardant suit and cape.

"I can explain on camera," she told him. "But I just want to deliver a message. With no follow-up questions. This won't be an interview."

"Of course," said the news director. "Tom, give her your seat."

The male news anchor did as he was told, looking a bit put out, and Supergirl took his place with an apologetic smile.

"Barbara will do the lead-in for the message," said the news director, nodding to the female anchor. "Supergirl, you'll look into this camera right here." He pointed to one directly in front of her. "And let us know when you're ready to go."

Supergirl nodded and took a few steadying breaths, collecting her thoughts. "Ready."

The cameraman pointed at Barbara, and the female news anchor smiled broadly. "Ladies and gentlemen, we are live with a surprise guest to our news program." She gestured to Supergirl. "The one and only Supergirl, with a message for the people of National City."

Supergirl smiled at the news anchor. "Thank you, Barbara." She faced the camera and dropped her smile. "Strange things have been happening in National City today, as many of you know. Ordinary citizens have been developing superpowers and testing them." Out of the corner of her eye, she could see Barbara scribbling furiously on a notepad.

"Unfortunately," Supergirl continued, "these supercitizens, as they're being called, don't really know what they're getting into. Many are overwhelmed by their powers and haven't mastered them. This is how the big cats escaped from the zoo and why there was a busted water pipe at the natural springs."

Barbara started to speak but caught herself.

"I've spoken with a couple supercitizens," said Supergirl, "but for the ones I haven't talked to, please hear me." Her brow furrowed. "Don't risk your lives or the lives of others playing with your powers. They may not be permanent, but the damage you could cause will be. Barbara?" Supergirl looked to her left, and the camera panned to the startled female news anchor, her pen poised over her notepad.

"Thank—thank you, Supergirl," Barbara said, speaking into the camera. "You'd mentioned this wasn't an interview, but I'd still like to ask a few questions." She swiveled in her seat, but the chair beside her was empty, and Supergirl was already halfway to the exit.

Feeling pretty pleased, Supergirl sprang from the tenth-floor balcony and took off into the night sky.

"Winn, I'm on my way!" she said.

"Uh, OK," he said in a tense voice. "But you should stop and pick up a bag of Chocos for J'onn," he replied.

"Chocos cookies?" Supergirl asked with a frown. "Why?"

"He just saw your live broadcast," said Winn. "And he's pretty mad."

# 7

THERE WERE TIMES WHEN ALEX envied her little sister and all the attention she got.

This particular moment was not one of them.

As soon as Winn pulled up the video of Supergirl addressing the supercitizens, J'onn crushed his coffee mug, spilling coffee and broken glass all over Winn's desk.

Winn yelped as scalding coffee trickled into his lap, and scrambled out of his chair.

"Dude! What gives?" He scowled at J'onn, who scowled right back. Winn swallowed hard. "I mean . . . is everything OK? Boss?"

Instead of answering, J'onn whirled on Alex. "What is your sister thinking? Does she have any idea what she's done?"

Alex didn't as much as flinch under his relentless glare. She'd been on the receiving end of his outbursts more than a few times, and she knew they never ended in harm to her. Coffee mugs, on the other hand . . .

"She's just protecting the supercitizens from themselves," Alex told him.

"And exposing them to all of National City. Possibly the world!" J'onn pointed to the news broadcast. "The DEO is about secrecy and security. What part of that has Supergirl forgotten?" J'onn chucked the remains of his coffee mug into a trash can.

Winn cleared his throat. "Not to be the guy who disagrees with his boss, but pretty much everyone in National City already knows." His fingers flew across the keyboard, and in minutes the video wall was flooded with Tweets, Instas, and other social media posts that mentioned supercitizen sightings. "If you look at the time stamps, these are all from *before* Supergirl's speech."

Alex studied J'onn, whose forehead was still wrinkled into peaks and valleys. "That's not the only thing bothering you about this, is it?"

J'onn held up his index finger. "I said the DEO is about secrecy, but I also said it's about security." He lifted a second finger, and Alex nodded.

"And Supergirl *is* concerned about the security of

everyone in National City," she said. "That's why she asked the supercitizens to stand down."

J'onn shook his head. "She didn't ask them, Alex." He pointed to the floor. "She drew a line in the sand and dared them to cross it."

"But they won't cross it," said Alex.

J'onn scoffed. "Some of them won't. What about those who do?"

Alex shrugged. "We'll take care of them."

J'onn's expression didn't lighten. "I'm going to check on James and Mon-El. If we can find an antidote for this nightmare, maybe we won't have to worry about the fallout from it."

He stormed off toward the infirmary, where James and Mon-El were being examined. Or rather, James and a Japanese man who claimed to be Mon-El. When the two had arrived at the DEO, James had told everyone he and Mon-El had gotten new powers like the supercitizens. James then asked to borrow two quarters he could see in Winn's closed desk drawer. The Japanese man with James had lifted the snack machine over his head and shaken a bag of chips free.

He definitely acted like Mon-El, at least.

With an exasperated sigh, Alex followed J'onn into the infirmary, where James was reading an eye chart from across the room . . . while facing the opposite direction.

"Amazing." The physician, Dr. Hoshi, jotted a note. "How about with your eyes closed?"

James did as she asked and read the eye chart again, this time from the bottom to the top.

"Are we sure he doesn't just have the thing memorized?" Alex asked with a smirk.

James grinned. "Don't believe me? You've got a roll of breath mints in your pocket," he said, squinting at Alex's jacket. "Wintergreen."

Alex crossed her arms over herself and frowned. "Stop that."

"How's the DNA analysis going?" J'onn asked Dr. Hoshi.

"It's taking longer than we'd hoped," she confessed. "We know nearsightedness and color blindness have associations with certain chromosomes. But supersight that includes the ability to see through objects, to see things behind your head, and in total darkness?" Dr. Hoshi shook her head. "That's unprecedented."

"You can see in the dark?" Alex asked James. "That's pretty cool."

From an examination table in the corner, Mon-El groaned. "Can we stop talking about him for one second and focus on me?"

Everyone turned their attention to the grumpy Daxamite in the Japanese scientist's body.

"How much longer am I going to be like this?" he asked.

Dr. Hoshi sighed. "That's harder to tell than with Mr. Olsen. I can't even get a needle into your skin to pull a blood sample." She paused and wrinkled her forehead. "Not that I'm entirely sure I can splice alien DNA. But I'll see if I can find *something* to penetrate your skin."

"At least you still sound like yourself," Alex told a pouting Mon-El as Dr. Hoshi left the room. "If we turned out the lights, we wouldn't even know you'd changed."

"Well, I would," James said with a chuckle.

Alex smacked his arm. "Not helping."

"So James has supersight," said J'onn. "And Mon-El can change his appearance." He looked from one of them to the other. "Do either of you know how this happened?"

"I think this might have something to do with it." James pulled a thimble-sized jar from his pocket, the contents of which clinked against the glass container.

J'onn took it from him and held it up to the light.

Inside the jar was a scrap of metal that looked like iron, but with a reddish tint.

"We found it at Dr. Wanabi's apartment," said James. "Along with *that*." He nodded toward a spiral-bound notebook on a side table.

J'onn put the jar on the table and glanced at the notebook. "It's in Japanese."

Alex pressed the intercom button. "Winn, can you come to the infirmary?"

"Be right there!" he responded.

Alex picked up the jar containing the metal. "So what do we think this is? Some form of red kryptonite?" she asked.

"Nope. I'd definitely feel it," said a voice from the doorway.

Supergirl.

Alex pressed her lips together and shot J'onn a warning look, but he was already advancing on the Girl of Steel.

"I am *not* happy about that little TV stunt you pulled," he growled. "Do you realize what you've done?"

"Yes, I've stopped a bunch of power-happy people from destroying the city." Supergirl held up the bag of Chocos. "Cookie?"

"I'll take one!" Mon-El hopped off his examination table. "How was your day, babe?" He leaned in to kiss Supergirl, and Alex cringed.

Because Mon-El had apparently forgotten he looked like someone else.

"Whoa!" Supergirl ducked out of his reach. "Back off, dude. I have a boyfriend."

Mon-El's forehead wrinkled. "*Another* boyfriend? First the guy at Noonan's, now this? How many other men are you dating?"

Alex cleared her throat. "Mon-El?" She held up a steel surgical tray so he could see his reflection.

"Oh, right." He chuckled. "I keep forgetting."

Supergirl, who'd been clutching the bag of Chocos like a protective shield, let it fall to the floor. "You're Mon-El? My Mon-El?"

He held his arms open. "In the flesh! So to speak."

"What . . . happened?" Supergirl touched his cheeks with both hands.

"James and I visited Shady Oaks apartments, and we got hit by some weird substance. Probably the same thing that gave the residents superpowers," said Mon-El.

Alex shook the jar containing the red metal. "We think it was this."

Supergirl looked from Mon-El to James. "You were both affected? James, what's your superpower?"

James glanced at the wall beside Supergirl. "Winn's about to walk through that door."

He pointed to the infirmary entrance, and a second later, Winn entered. Supergirl stared, openmouthed, and Winn froze.

"What? Do I have something on my face?" He reached up and wiped his nose.

Supergirl turned to James. "You have X-ray vision, like me?"

"X-ray vision, exceptionally enhanced peripheral vision, night vision." He started ticking them off on his fingers.

Mon-El made a scoffing sound. "Yeah, but he can't alter his appearance. That takes real talent." He popped his collar.

Supergirl shook her head. "How—"

"Excuse me!" J'onn spoke up, frowning. "We're not done discussing that broadcast you made," he told Supergirl.

For the second time that night, Alex had to endure a speech about the many ways her sister had screwed up. The longer J'onn spoke, the tighter Supergirl crossed her arms. If he was trying to convince Supergirl she was wrong, it wasn't working.

"First of all," Supergirl said when he'd finally finished, "it's too late to change what I did. Unless you want me to, I don't know, fly around the Earth a bunch and reverse time."

Winn clucked his tongue. "Yeahhh. I don't think that would actually work."

"Second of all," Supergirl ignored Winn, "everyone was bound to find out about the supercitizens. We live in an age where everything's on the Internet ."

"Plus, you told every media outlet during the Reyes interview," Winn said out of the corner of his mouth.

This time Supergirl fixed him with a look before continuing. "And I didn't challenge the supercitizens. If they feel like they've got something to prove, it's not because of me."

"Of *course* it's because of you!" J'onn exclaimed. "You're their idol! They want to be you. I see little kids running around wearing capes all the time."

"Then if they really look up to me, they'll listen." Supergirl gave a firm nod.

Mon-El put a hand on Supergirl's shoulder. "I think I understand what she's trying to say."

But nobody was paying attention to Mon-El's interpretation of Supergirl's words. They were all too busy staring at him.

As Mon-El spoke, his appearance as Dr. Wanabi changed.

He grew several inches, and his torso and face slimmed down. Instead of short, dark hair, he now had a mane of long blond hair that cascaded around his shoulders—shoulders covered by a red cape. His brown eyes brightened and turned blue, and when he pointed to himself, he pointed to a symbol of the House of El stamped on his chest.

Mon-El still sounded like himself but now looked exactly like Supergirl.

The real Supergirl, who'd been glowering at J'onn, was the next to last to notice, and when she glanced at Mon-El, she jumped.

"Jeez! What are you doing?" she asked.

"I'm being supportive of my girlfriend," he said, taking in all the awestruck faces around him. "Was that wrong?"

In answer, Alex held up the steel tray again, and Mon-El did a double take at his reflection.

"Oh, crap," he said.

Winn cleared his throat. "You know, they say after a while couples start to resemble each other."

James hid a smile. "You guys just took it to the next level."

The two Supergirls faced each other.

"I swear I didn't do this on purpose," said Mon-El. "I just wanted to connect with you."

Supergirl tilted her head to one side and grinned at him. "Really?"

"Well, yeah," he said, taking her hands.

J'onn massaged his forehead. "This is deeply disturbing."

While the Supergirls made googly eyes at each other, Alex mulled over Mon-El's words and thought back to the supercitizens the DEO had identified so far.

Mon-El had taken on Supergirl's appearance to connect with her, and lately he'd been interested in learning more about humans so he could understand them.

"Focus!" Alex blurted.

Everyone looked at her.

"Focus on what?" asked Supergirl.

Alex shook her head. "That's why the supercitizens get the powers they do. We almost had it right earlier today.

It's whatever they're focused on, whatever they're passionate about."

"So James is focused on seeing?" asked Winn.

Now everyone looked at James.

He ran a hand over his shaved scalp and tucked his chin. "When Mon-El and I went to Shady Oaks apartments, he noticed things I didn't—things I wished I'd seen." He chuckled. "I guess I must have been more focused on it than I thought."

"Wait. So you got your power because you were jealous of me?" Mon-El asked with a grin.

James gave him a withering look. "Don't read too much into it."

J'onn paced the room. "So we know who gets powers, why they get them, and where they get them." He indicated the jar of red metal Alex was holding. "But we don't know how they get them."

"Or when they'll lose them," said Supergirl.

"Or why you called me in here," added Winn, waving a hand.

Alex smacked herself on the forehead. "Right! Sorry, Winn. James and Mon-El found a notebook in Dr. Wanabi's apartment." She nodded to J'onn, who handed it to Winn. "Can you use translation software to find out what it says?"

"Absolutely." Winn took his phone from his back pocket

and snapped a picture of the first page. He tapped a few buttons on the screen and waited. "It looks like scientific formulas." Winn's eyes flitted across the screen. "Yikes! It also looks like the first one was a huge failure. It's crossed out in red with 'explosive' written beside it."

"The landlady at Shady Oaks mentioned there was an explosion," spoke up James.

"And shortly after that, everyone in Dr. Wanabi's building developed superpowers," said Supergirl.

"Everyone on floors three and up," corrected Mon-El. "Based on our talk with Dr. Wanabi."

J'onn exchanged a look with Alex. "How much are you willing to bet that after the explosion, particles of that metal went—"

"Airborne?" Alex finished for him. She looked at Mon-El and James. "Did either of you touch that red metal directly?"

They both shook their heads, and J'onn and Alex exchanged another glance. This time, of satisfaction.

"As long as we quarantine that apartment complex and keep this stuff under lock and key"—Alex held up the jar— "we don't have to worry about any more supercitizens."

"I'll make some calls," said J'onn—at the same time an alarm sounded overhead. He pointed to Alex. "You check on that."

She nodded. "Winn?"

"I'm on it," he said, closing the translation screen on his phone and pulling up the DEO's security matrix. "Looks like it's coming from Bubbles's cell."

Alex motioned to Supergirl. "Let's go see what our fishy friend is up to."

"I'll come with you," said Mon-El, flinging his cape over one shoulder.

Alex looked him over and smirked. "No thanks, *sis*. I want you and James to use Winn's camera cogitari and think about your visit to Shady Oaks. Hopefully, we can fill in some missing details."

"Use Winn's what?" asked James.

Winn gestured toward the door. "Follow me, gentlemen."

Alex and Supergirl let them pass before stepping into the hall, and Supergirl watched Mon-El with a curious expression.

"I've never seen myself run before," she said. "Do I always look that weird?"

Alex laughed. "Mon-El only has your exterior appearance. Everything else is totally him."

Supergirl made a face. "Then don't tell him I said that."

The Danvers sisters hurried to Bubbles's cell, where overhead strobe lights flashed in sync with the warning buzzer.

Alex pressed her hand to the scanner, and when she and Supergirl entered the room, they saw Bubbles's tank . . . but no Bubbles.

"Uh-oh," said Supergirl, glancing around.

Alex pressed an intercom button beside the closing cell door. "Winn, I need a location update on Bubbles. He's not in here."

There was silence from the other end for a moment. Then, "Uh . . . yeah, he is."

"What?" said Alex, at the same moment the wall beside the intercom started to move.

"Alex, look out!" shouted Supergirl.

Bubbles lunged for Alex, his skin the color and appearance of the wall he'd blended into.

He'd set a trap, and she and Supergirl had walked right into it.

Alex crouched and rolled to the side to avoid Bubbles's grasp as Supergirl launched herself at him, fists raised.

Bubbles pressed himself against the wall, and Supergirl smirked.

"You can't hide this time!" she said.

But Bubbles didn't even try to blend in. Instead, he seemed to be anticipating Supergirl's attack.

And that was when Alex realized he was standing in front of the lighting panel.

"Kara, wait!" she shouted, forgetting discretion.

It was too late.

Just as Supergirl's fist was about to strike Bubbles's face, he stepped to the side. The lighting panel received the force of Supergirl's punch, and after a shower of sparks and metal shrapnel, the room went dark.

"Alex?" Supergirl's voice came from behind her.

Alex didn't answer. She couldn't risk Bubbles finding her by sound, and she knew Supergirl could hear her heartbeat. That would have to be enough to satisfy her sister.

Sinking low to the floor, Alex let her other senses compensate for her lack of sight. She heard a whoosh and a flapping sound: her sister, flying up to the ceiling. Alex inhaled and smelled the sea. Bubbles was close by.

Then, suddenly, footsteps thundered toward her, and the scent of the ocean grew stronger. Bubbles was running at her full tilt. Clearly, he had no trouble seeing in the dark.

Alex straightened and sprinted for the center of the room, taking off her jacket. "Supergirl! I need you to start a fire!" she shouted, swinging her jacket in front of her until it smacked against the fish tank wall.

"With what?" Supergirl shouted back.

"My jacket! At the center of the room!" Alex dropped it and sprinted away just as twin beams of blue light cut the darkness where she'd been.

Supergirl's heat vision roved the floor for a second until it fell upon Alex's jacket, which instantly ignited.

The fire wasn't much, but it was enough to see by, and enough for the fight to be a little fairer.

Bubbles swung a fist at Alex, who veered to the side and landed a punch of her own to the creature's rib cage. Bubbles grunted but didn't go down. Still, it was good to know he was vulnerable.

Alex stepped back and raised a leg, kicking out hard. Bubbles caught her foot between his hands and twisted, flipping Alex in midair so that she was headed face-first for the floor. Alex threw out her hands to stop herself, and as soon as her palms touched the ground, she kicked back with her free leg, connecting with Bubbles's stomach.

He dropped her other foot and she scrambled away, turning over just as Supergirl flew down and slugged Bubbles. His head turned to one side, but the blow didn't drop him. Supergirl's eyes widened in surprise as he grabbed her by the throat and carried her, clawing and kicking, to the cell door.

Now Alex understood.

Bubbles had seen the DEO members use the hand scanner to exit the room, and now he wanted to do the same. He just needed someone's hand.

Alex chased after him and jumped on his back, digging her fingers into the arm holding Supergirl and hoping that sea monsters had pressure points, too. She squeezed his wrist with all her might, and felt Bubbles's grip relax. With a greedy gasp for air, Supergirl dropped to the floor while Bubbles reached back for Alex and flung her up and over his head.

This time, she didn't catch herself.

Alex struck the wall and then the floor, her right arm and back throbbing.

But there was no rest for the wounded.

Bubbles grabbed Alex's left arm and dragged her toward the hand scanner by the door. Through her dim, star-scattered vision, Alex spotted the tablet computer in its holster.

With a Herculean effort, she hauled herself to her feet and reached for the tablet with her injured arm, pain slicing through her. She whipped the tablet backward and caught Bubbles across the windpipe.

He coughed and gasped, letting go of Alex and reaching for his throat.

Out of the corner of her eye, Alex saw her sister shooting across the room and stepped aside, happy to let her finish the task.

"Fish out of water!" Supergirl said, grabbing Bubbles under the arms and lifting him into the air.

Alex placed her hand against the door scanner, and light

from the hallway flooded the room. Several DEO agents stormed in, guns drawn.

"You OK, Danvers?" one of them asked.

Alex nodded and rested her back against the doorframe while Supergirl dropped Bubbles into his tank.

"I know you can't understand me," Supergirl told him. "But I'll bet you can figure out what they'll do if you try to escape again." She pointed to the DEO agents, and with an angry screech, Bubbles sank to the bottom of his tank.

Supergirl zipped over to Alex and took her sister in her arms. "Are you OK?"

Alex patted her on the back. "Nothing a hot bath and a new body won't fix."

J'onn sprinted down the hall toward them. "Alex!"

"I'm OK," she said, waving him off. "But we need to keep a closer eye on Bubbles. He's craftier—and a way better fighter—than we gave him credit for."

"I'm taking Alex home," Supergirl told J'onn.

He nodded. "Once you're done, I'll need you back so we can talk about the repercussions of your broadcast."

Supergirl shook her head. "Not now. We'll deal with it when it happens. And it won't be that bad."

"I hope you're right," he said as Supergirl and Alex walked away. "For the sake of everyone in National City."

# 8

**H**APPY TUESDAY, NATIONAL CITY! *Our top headline: Supergirl sucks!"*

Kara's eyes shot open as she heard the radio coming from her neighbor's apartment. She fumbled for her own clock radio and tuned to the same frequency.

*". . . message found burned into the grass in Pineda Park this morning. After Supergirl begged supercitizens to stand down, the response has been less than cooperative and less than friendly. In addition to the lit-up lawn, supercitizens have created and destroyed an effigy of the Girl of Steel, skewered with no fewer than a dozen swords."*

"Seriously?" Kara glared at her radio, searing it with her heat vision until it smoked and fell silent. With a grunt, she fluffed her pillow and pulled the covers over her head.

While Kara silently fumed, someone knocked at her front door.

"Kara?" Alex's voice carried into the apartment.

Kara wanted to ignore her sister, but with her X-ray vision, she could see that Alex had brought coffee and a box of doughnuts.

"It's not fair that you know all my weaknesses!" she informed Alex, trudging to the front door.

"These are a thank-you for taking me home last night and not telling Maggie what happened," said Alex, holding a cup of coffee out to her sister. "If she knew I let a prisoner trick me, I'd never hear the end of it."

"Glad to help." Kara took the coffee and stepped aside so her sister could enter. "How's Mon-El doing?"

J'onn had wanted to keep him and James overnight for observation, which had been a relief to Kara. She couldn't have imagined spending an evening with Mon-El while he looked like her.

"He's looking like himself again," said Alex. "It happened after he fell asleep. His powers must be controlled at the conscious level."

"Oh, thank Rao!" Kara praised the Kryptonian diety while taking the lid off her coffee cup. "I love the smell of caffeine in the morning."

"It's definitely better than whatever you've been cooking in here," said Alex, wrinkling her nose.

Kara swallowed a mouthful of coffee. "My radio. It gave me bad news, so I killed it."

Alex raised an eyebrow. "Then you might not want to check your phone. Or your television. Or any newsstands."

"What?" Despite her sister's warning, Kara turned on the television.

A news broadcast showed footage of a boy and girl who looked almost identical sitting on the back of an unconscious man in a ski mask. These "wonder twins," as the newscaster called them, were holding a sign that read, WHO NEEDS SUPERGIRL?

"Oh, come on!" Kara dropped onto her sofa. "Why are people being such jerks about this? I was trying to do a good thing, Alex."

"I know you were, sweetie." Alex sat beside her. "But remember when you first became Supergirl? I told you never to use your powers, and you did anyway."

Kara narrowed her eyes at her sister. "If you're trying to compare me to the supercitizens, this is *worlds* different. For starters, I never wrote 'Alex sucks' on the lawn at the park!"

"No, but you probably thought it," Alex said with a smirk.

Kara sighed and pulled a cruller from the box of doughnuts, cramming it in her mouth. "J'onn knows about all this, doesn't he?" she mumbled around a mouthful of cruller.

Alex sucked in her breath. "That's why I'm here. He wanted to make sure you wouldn't take any action against the supercitizens."

Kara snorted and swallowed. "Any action? What, like sue them?"

Alex tilted her hand from side to side. "That, or fly them to your family's Fortress of Solitude and leave them for dead."

Kara shook her head. "I've got bigger things to worry about." She reached down and picked up her cell phone, which vibrated with a text from Snapper Carr. "Like not losing my job again." She polished off her coffee and grabbed one last doughnut. "Thank you for breakfast, and tell J'onn he has nothing to worry about."

"Isn't that what you told him last night?" Alex called as Kara walked to her bedroom.

"Aren't you supposed to be on my side?" Kara retorted. She zipped into a gray sheath dress and pink cardigan, hopping back to the living room as she pulled on a pair of flats.

"I'm always on your side," Alex assured her, handing Kara her phone while she grabbed her purse. "See you at the DEO later?"

Kara nodded and followed her out the front door. "Make sure J'onn gets all his gloating done before I show up."

• • •

Kara shouldn't have been surprised that James was back behind his desk at CatCo, but she froze when she saw him anyway. She knew how much James had wanted a feature on up-and-coming superheroes, and now, thanks to what J'onn had called "repercussions," supercitizens were all over every form of media. If CatCo didn't jump on board, it'd be the only major news brand left behind.

Kara joined the other journalists gathered in James's office, all of whom were watching him argue with Snapper.

". . . a fad," Snapper was saying. "And a ridiculous one at that."

"Well, it's all anyone can talk about right now," said James. "And if we don't, we lose. So we need to be all over this." He raised his voice so everyone could hear him. "*Tribune* reporters, I want you listening in on police scanners. If anything sounds even remotely supercitizen related, we should be the first on the scene."

Half the gathered group murmured their assent and left.

"Magazine journos, Snapper has a bunch of new features for you to work on. If we hurry, we can have them online tonight!" James clapped his hands. "Let's get moving, people!"

Snapper pushed his way through the crowd, but when

he tried to shoulder past Kara, she didn't budge. Snapper stumbled back a few paces.

"Jeez, Ponytail!" He rubbed his shoulder. "You practicing to be a roadblock?"

"We're not doing an entire magazine issue on the supercitizens, are we?" she asked in response.

Snapper's scowl lightened to an expression of surprise. "I would've pegged you to be on Olsen's side. But yeah, it's starting to look that way." He glanced back at James and glowered. "I have half a mind to write another opinion piece in the *Tribune*," he muttered.

It was Kara's turn to be surprised. "You wrote an op-ed for the *Tribune*?"

Snapper's face was back to its usual dark expression. "You don't think I should have an opinion?"

Kara shook her head. "It's not that. I just . . . what was the op-ed about?"

"How print isn't dead," said Snapper, walking to his desk. "The public library near my house is closing down, and I wanted to save it." He cupped his hands around his mouth. "Investigative journos at my desk!"

Kara didn't joke about being the first one there again. She was too busy thinking about Snapper's op-ed on the library. It reminded her of something . . .

"Danvers, you're covering superdrugs." Snapper's voice cut into her thoughts.

"Sorry, superdrugs?" Kara pushed her glasses up the bridge of her nose. "As in antibiotics?"

Snapper stared at her unblinkingly. "Superdrugs, as in drugs that give people superpowers. Ever since Supergirl's speech last night, half the city wants them."

"I'm all over it." She gave him a thumbs-up.

"Start at Hillside Pharmacy," he told her. "I've heard through the grapevine that the pharmacist there has a connection."

"Got it!" she said and headed for James's office.

"Ponytail, the exit's that way," said Snapper, pointing to the elevator.

Kara laughed nervously. "Oh yeah, I know. I just need to ask James something, uh, personal."

Snapper rolled his eyes and went back to addressing the rest of his team. Luckily, they were too wrapped up to see Kara punch James in the arm.

"Ow! You're not supposed to superpunch the good guys!" he whispered harshly, rubbing his injury. "What was *that* for?"

"If I'm trying to keep the supercitizens from using their powers, why are you trying to draw attention *to* them?" she asked.

James sighed and sat on the edge of his desk. "Look, Kara, you know I respect your opinions, but you're not the only hero around here." He gestured to the television screens behind him, most of which featured a supercitizen report. "I just want to give recognition where it's due."

Kara shook her head. "You should *not* be encouraging this. I had to repair the city's plumbing last night because of a supercitizen. And there were lions roaming the streets because of another one!"

"Funny." James crossed his arms. "I seem to recall you causing an oil spill when you first started saving this city."

Kara felt her cheeks warm. "That's . . . I . . ."

He pointed at her. "And didn't you also turn Leslie Willis into Livewire while trying to save her traffic chopper?"

Kara clenched her fists at her side. "Both of those were accidents!"

James chuckled. "And you think these supercitizens are screwing up on purpose?"

Kara set her jaw and adjusted her glasses. "You know what? I can't have this conversation right now. I have a pharmacist to stop."

She turned on her heel and stormed away, with James calling after her, "Think about it, Kara!"

Not bothering with the elevator, she pushed open the door to the fire stairs and flew up to the roof and across town to Hillside Pharmacy. She didn't even care if anyone saw.

But while she'd been quick to arrive, now that she was in front of the building, Kara took her time walking in. Hillside Pharmacy wasn't quite what she expected.

Instead of a brick-and-mortar building, the pharmacy was a mobile trailer hitched to a truck, as if it were prepared to leave town at a moment's notice. The outside was painted green with peeling red letters that read ILLSIDE PHARMAC.

"Who'd buy medicine here?" she wondered aloud. "Who'd buy *anything* here?"

The trailer door stuck when she opened it, and she pulled hard enough to shake the entire structure. A bell jangled above the door, but it wasn't necessary. She could see from one end of the trailer to the other, where the pharmacist sat. He was an older man with a bowed back and more hair coming from his ears than the top of his head.

"Can I help you, miss?" he asked.

Kara smiled and strolled over shyly. "I've heard you carry . . . special supplies here."

The pharmacist frowned. "Special supplies?"

Kara leaned forward and whispered. "Supplies that can make people *super*."

The pharmacist grinned. "Ahhh. You mean Power Powder."

He opened a cabinet mounted to the wall and pulled out a jar filled with purple powder.

Purple.

But the mysterious metal from Dr. Wanabi's apartment was red.

"Drink one spoonful of this mixed into a glass of water and you'll be just like Supergirl," said the pharmacist.

Kara feigned fascination. "Really?"

The pharmacist nodded. "Of course, the effects take a few days to kick in."

*Of course they do*, Kara thought. *Long enough for you to collect your money and get out of town.*

"I recommend a minimum of four doses for full effect," the pharmacist continued.

Kara didn't bat an eyelash. "How much does each dose cost?"

"Thirty dollars."

"Wow!" Kara smiled at the pharmacist. "Who could pass that up?"

The pharmacist chuckled. "Nobody has so far. And I've seen fifty people already today."

Kara chuckled, too. Then she grabbed the jar of powder from the pharmacist.

"Hey! Give that—owww!" he cried as Kara twisted his arm with one hand.

"What's *really* in this jar?" she asked.

"I told you!" the pharmacist gasped. "Power Powder!"

"Which is actually . . . ?" she prompted, twisting his arm even further.

"G-gelatin!" he shouted. "It's grape gelatin!"

Kara let the pharmacist go, and he collapsed on the floor, whimpering.

"You're going to start the truck attached to this trailer," said Kara, kneeling beside him, "and you're going to leave National City right now. Or I'll show you what real power can do." She crushed the jar of grape gelatin mix in one hand. "Understand?"

The pharmacist nodded and scooted away from her.

Kara straightened and opened the trailer door. "You should also fix your sign. You spelled 'con artist' wrong."

Slamming the door behind her, Kara stepped onto the sidewalk and headed for the nearest alley. She needed to fly back to the DEO straightaway.

What if it hadn't been grape gelatin people were drinking? What if it'd been rat poison? They were forking over their money just for a taste of power—no matter the price. The worst part was that this "pharmacist" probably wasn't the only one selling fake formulas.

Kara paused. No, the worst part was knowing that J'onn was right.

Her speech as Supergirl had brought chaos to National City before it was ready. Yes, people had been aware of super-citizens, but being publicized by Supergirl had made them famous. And others craved the same fame, which made them search for superpowers, turning to strangers who were eager to take advantage of them.

Ducking between two Dumpsters, Kara leaped into the air and rocketed across the city. When she walked into the DEO control room, Alex, J'onn, and Winn all glanced at her.

"Hey," she said, clasping her hands in front of her. "You've probably noticed the damage a certain video has caused today." She glanced at her feet before looking up at J'onn, who was studying her with arms crossed. "I'm sorry I didn't listen. How do we fix it?"

Instead of scolding Kara, J'onn turned back to the monitors. "We don't know yet. The mutated cells we retrieved from James's blood haven't shown signs of weakening or changing, and when we quarantined the apartment building, Dr. Wanabi was nowhere to be found."

Winn raised a hand. "But we *did* uncover a clue using the camera cogitari."

"The what?" Kara asked.

"It's a helmet that turns thoughts into images," explained Alex.

"*My* thoughts, thank you very much," said Mon-El from behind Kara.

She steeled herself for whatever version of him she might face, but luckily, he looked like himself.

"Mon-El! It's so good to see you!" Kara threw her arms around him. "The real you, I mean."

Mon-El squeezed her tight and chuckled. "You didn't like flirting with yourself yesterday?"

"I did that enough in high school," said Kara. At the strange looks from the other DEO agents, she hastily added, "In the mirror! I was practicing . . . You know what? It's not important." Kara cleared her throat and straightened her glasses. "What was the clue you found, Winn?"

With a few mouse clicks, he displayed an image on the video wall. "We nearly missed it. James and Mon-El saw almost the exact same things, but when Mon-El stopped to look at himself in a cabinet, we saw this . . ." Winn zoomed in on a picture frame resting on a shelf.

Kara squinted at the image. It appeared to be Dr. Wanabi with several friends, all in wet suits beneath a National City Marina sign.

"The image is a little blurry, but we're running facial recognition software on the men in the picture with Dr. Wanabi," said Alex. "We're hoping he might be staying with one of them."

The longer Kara stared at the image, the more something tugged at the back of her mind.

"I think this picture tells us more than who these men are," she said. "Where's that jar with the red metal in it?"

Alex furrowed her brow. "I've had it on me for safekeeping." She took it from her pocket and handed it to her sister.

"Thanks," said Kara. Without another word, she ran for the prison block.

"Wait! Where are you going?" Alex called after her.

"Miss Danvers!" bellowed J'onn.

Kara stopped in front of Bubbles's cell and placed her hand on the scanner. When she entered the room, the guards inside raised their weapons, and just as quickly lowered them. In the center of the room, Bubbles ceased swimming and floated in place, watching her intently.

Kara approached the tank and raised the jar of red metal where Bubbles could see it. "You know what this is, don't you?"

Bubbles's eyes widened, and he pounded against the wall of his tank.

"Aha! I thought so." Kara smiled triumphantly. "This is why you're here!" She shook the jar so that metal clinked against glass.

Bubbles continued to pound on the wall.

"Careful, ma'am," said one of the agents. "I think you're upsetting the creature."

"Kara!" Alex shouted. "What are you doing?"

"I know how Dr. Wanabi found this mysterious red metal," Kara told her. "He and his wet suit buddies stole it from Bubbles!" She faced the sea creature. "That's right, isn't it? This is yours?" She pointed from the jar to him.

Bubbles screeched and kicked at the glass wall.

"Uh, Kara?" Winn tapped on the tablet computer. "You might want to back away from the tank."

She was too excited to listen. Kara opened the jar and let the red metal fall into her palm.

"Kara . . ." Alex said in a warning voice.

"Kara, don't touch that," said Mon-El. "That's concentrated, uh"—he fumbled for the right word—"stuff!"

She held her hand out to Bubbles. "Let's make a deal—"

But Kara never got to finish her bargain. Bubbles reeled back both legs and gave one last kick to his tank wall. The glass shattered to pieces. Salt water gushed through every open space, knocking Kara and the others off their feet and carrying them across the room.

Bubbles swam through the deluge of water and grabbed Kara's hand. Prying the red metal from her fingers, he flung it away and showed her a welt forming on her palm.

"Poison," he said, looking her in the eyes. "Poison and power."

# 9

THE SKIN ON KARA'S PALM TIGHTENED and blistered, but she was too shocked to register the pain.

"Did . . . did you just say something?" she asked Bubbles. She splashed to a sitting position in the knee-deep water filling the room. "You said poison and power, didn't you?"

Bubbles regarded her with wide eyes. "You understand me?"

Kara chuckled. "Well, yeah. When you speak English."

"Uhhh, Kara?" Mon-El crouched in the water beside her. "What are you doing?"

Kara beamed at Mon-El while pointing at Bubbles. "Look who can finally talk! It's . . ." She paused and whispered to Bubbles, "I'm sorry. What was your name?"

"Pryll," the sea creature supplied.

"It's Pryll!" Kara gestured to him as if he were a contestant on a game show.

From nearby, Winn cleared his throat. "Actually, I think Mon-El's referring to the thing you're doing with the . . ." He took a deep breath and screeched.

"What?" Kara laughed. "I'm not making that sound." She glanced at the rest of the team, but nobody agreed with her. Kara's forehead wrinkled. "Am I?"

"You sound like a sick dolphin," Alex spoke up. "But Pryll seems to understand you." She gestured at him.

Kara got to her feet. "Wait a minute. Are you saying I can speak . . . whatever language Pryll can?" She turned to Pryll, who was also getting to his feet. "You can understand me?"

He nodded.

Kara pointed at Mon-El. "But *you* couldn't understand that?"

Mon-El shook his head.

Kara's mouth dropped open and she whirled on Pryll, who jumped back, startled.

"What language are we speaking?" she asked.

Pryll eyed her warily. "Atlantean."

With a laugh, Kara clutched a hand to her chest. "I speak Atlantean!"

"Wait, wait, wait." Winn waved his hands. "Atlantean? As in the lost city of Atlantis?" He ran a tongue over his teeth and smirked at Alex. "So it *does* exist."

Alex ignored him. "Kara, how do you suddenly speak Atlantean?"

"It must be this!" Kara showed Alex the palm that had been holding the red metal, and Alex recoiled, averting her gaze.

"Oh, God. That . . . that is a very big blister." She pointed at Kara's hand.

"Huh?" Kara glanced at her palm, which looked much worse than it had moments ago. "Eesh. So much for impervious skin."

Mon-El snuck a peek at Kara's hand, and his eyes widened. "The red metal did that?" He ran his hands over his arms and touched his chest. "I breathed it in! What's it doing to *me*?"

Kara frowned. "Pryll said 'poison and power.' What did you mean by that?" She faced Pryll, who tilted his head quizzically, and she realized he'd understood only half the conversation. "What did you mean by poison and power?" she asked again, focusing her attention on him.

"The orichalcum gives great power," said Pryll, "but poisons the body, mind, and soul of those who use it. In the age of Atlantis, it caused much pain and sorrow."

Kara translated for the DEO team, and J'onn frowned.

"How much poison would that be exactly?" he asked.

Kara relayed the question to Pryll.

"The more one consumes, the more one is poisoned," said the Atlantean. He pointed to Kara's hand. "That amount will not kill, but it will cause much pain."

Kara sighed and spoke to J'onn. "If the supercitizens only breathed dust from the apartment explosion, they shouldn't suffer too much, but *I'm* in for some rough nights."

"Maybe not," said Alex. "He's assuming you're human. The orichalcum might not affect you the same." Alex shook her head. "What I don't get is why Pryll is suddenly acting so calm. Yesterday he almost killed us trying to escape."

"I'm sure it makes a difference that we can communicate," said Kara. "But I'll ask."

She turned toward Pryll again, and J'onn stepped between them.

"If I may, I'd like to try creating a mental bridge," he told Kara. "Since you can understand Pryll, and I can understand you, I should be able to connect all our minds so we can communicate."

Kara's eyebrows went up. "Telepathically?"

J'onn nodded. "If this works."

Winn breathed in deep. "I'm going to mind-speak with

someone from Atlantis. This is awesooome!" he sang under his breath.

Alex touched J'onn's arm. "You can make mental bridges?"

"It's very taxing," J'onn admitted, "but since we're all in the same room, I should be able to hold the connection for a few minutes."

"Then we'll talk fast," said Kara. She spoke to Pryll. "My friend is going to mentally link us so we can all understand one another."

Pryll nodded, and Kara gave J'onn a thumbs-up. "Whenever you're ready," she said.

J'onn excused the DEO agents who had been guarding Pryll, while Alex pressed a button on the wall to drain the room. Once the water had been reduced to a few puddles, Kara found the piece of orichalcum that Pryll had knocked from her hand and scooped it back into the jar. It was much smaller in size now, and she shuddered, knowing the rest of it was coursing through her body.

J'onn instructed Kara and the others to form a tight circle around him, then closed his eyes.

"You may begin, Miss Danvers," he said.

Kara turned to Pryll and focused her thoughts. *Yesterday, when you tried to escape, you almost killed my sister and Supergirl.*

*Supergirl,* Pryll thought with another tilt of his head. *You refer to yourself in the third person?*

Everyone looked at Kara, who opened and closed her mouth several times. *No, I'm . . . I'm not Supergirl. Supergirl is—*

*You,* thought Pryll. *Without eye coverings.* He pointed to Kara's glasses.

"He's got her there," Winn spoke to Mon-El out of the corner of his mouth.

"I've always thought it was a terrible disguise," Mon-El whispered.

Kara gave them both a look. *You know I can hear you speaking* and *thinking, right?*

Winn and Mon-El fell quiet and stared at the floor.

*I am sorry if I caused you or your sister harm, Supergirl,* thought Pryll. *You were unfortunate enough to enter the room when I tried to escape. I cannot fulfill my duties trapped here.*

*What are your duties?* thought Alex.

*I am a guardian of Atlantis, charged with protecting the treasures of my city,* thought Pryll.

*Which were stolen,* thought Winn. He pulled up the image of the divers on his tablet, and Pryll nodded.

*I do not know the thieves—only what they wear,* thought Pryll. *But you have found some of what they took.* He pointed to the jar of orichalcum Kara was holding.

The others exchanged glances.

*Some?* thought Mon-El. *There's more of that stuff?*

*Ugh. Of course!* Alex enlarged the image on Winn's tablet screen to focus on the net the divers carried between them. *How could we have been so stupid? They're not hauling a tiny piece of orichalcum.*

*They're hauling an entire cache,* completed Kara.

*So where's the rest of it?* wondered Winn.

*That's the million-dollar question,* thought Alex.

*Dr. Wanabi wasn't keeping it at his apartment,* thought Mon-El. *James and I searched the entire place.*

*How did he come to own the piece in his possession?* thought Pryll.

*He must have kept it after the dive,* thought Kara. *But who did he give the rest to?*

*Maxwell Lord?* suggested Alex. *Lillian Luthor?*

*National City Museum,* thought Mon-El.

Kara snapped her fingers. *We saw those robbers who lived in Dr. Wanabi's apartment building there! And when you and James showed up at his apartment, he was expecting someone.*

Mon-El nodded. *Plus, I found this in my pocket.*

He held out a soggy pamphlet from the museum with a now-familiar image of Atlantis on the front beneath the words SPECIAL EXHIBIT: TREASURES OF THE DEEP.

"Winn? Can you confirm the orichalcum is at the museum?" Alex asked out loud.

"Let's see," he said, tapping on the tablet screen. "It looks like the museum took in several shipments the other day. One was a box from a printing company, one was a box from Sotheby's auction house, and one was a crate from Sea Kings Dive Company." He scrolled down the screen. "The manifest includes some drinking vessels, jewelry, coins . . ." He glanced up. "And several bars of red metal."

*If the orichalcum is at the museum,* Kara thought, *we have to get to it before Dr. Wanabi. I bet he's trying to find a way to replicate it.*

*I will accompany you,* thought Pryll.

Kara put out a hand to stop him. *I'm sorry, but I can't let you do that. It's already dangerous with so many people in this city running around with superpowers.*

Pryll puffed out his chest. *But I am a guardian of Atlantis, charged with protecting its treasures!*

*And I'm a guardian of National City,* Kara informed him. *Please let us handle this. We'll bring back your treasures. I promise.*

Pryll's entire body slumped in defeat.

"Uh, guys?" Winn said aloud, staring at the tablet. "I hacked into the museum's security feed. If you want to beat Dr. Wanabi to the orichalcum, you might want to hurry."

He showed them the screen. On it was an image of Dr. Wanabi standing near an exhibit and checking his watch.

"Let's go," said Alex, patting J'onn on the shoulder.

The DEO director stirred and opened his eyes, which were bloodshot and bleary. "I'm afraid I won't be much use to you right now. Best to take your sister, Mon-El, and James. And bring a strike team. Dr. Wanabi is obviously waiting for someone."

"I'll text James and have him meet you at the museum," said Winn.

Kara handed Winn the jar of orichalcum. "Don't let this *or* Pryll out of your sight," she said in a low voice. "And please don't use this under any circumstances."

Winn smirked. "Trust me, my only focus is technology, and I can't get more super at that than I already am."

Kara stared at Winn until he sighed and crossed his heart with his index finger.

"I won't use the orichalcum even if there's a dire emergency," he promised. "Although how cool would Winntastic be as a superhero name?"

Kara rolled her eyes and opened the cell door.

"Schottcaller?" he tried again. "No? What about Sureschott? The Winnonator!" he asked the others as they followed Kara out the door. "Guys, this is long overdue!"

# 10

WITH SUPERGIRL'S GIFT OF flight and Mon-El's superspeed, they were the first to arrive at the museum. When they entered the building, a security guard groaned and approached them.

"Not you two again," he said. "We just finished cleaning up from your last visit!"

"For which I gave you two verses of the apology song, Fred," Mon-El told the security guard. "But I see where this is going." He massaged his throat and hummed.

Supergirl rested a hand on Mon-El's arm to stop him. "Sir, if we don't catch the man who's about to steal one of your exhibits, there might not *be* a museum left for you to clean up," she told the security guard.

He gave Supergirl a dubious look. "Not possible. We've tightened security at all the exits and installed extra cameras. If something shady goes down, we'll spot it."

As he spoke the words, Supergirl heard an echo of his voice say something different.

*I know how to do my job, lady.*

Frowning, Supergirl stuck a finger in her ear and wiggled it. "Sorry, what did you say?"

"I said if something shady goes down, we'll spot it," Fred the security guard repeated. But again, there was an echo of his voice.

*I said I know how to do my job.*

Supergirl's eyebrows raised, and Mon-El nudged her. "You OK?"

"I think so." Supergirl felt a tingle in her palm. The one with the orichalcum scar.

With her new power, she wasn't just hearing the security guard's words; she was hearing what he really meant to say.

"I know you just want to do your job," she told him. "But right now, that means getting everyone out of the building quickly and quietly."

Fred didn't budge.

Supergirl sighed and turned to Mon-El, who stepped closer to the security guard.

"Look, Fred. This is an emergency, and you're the only

person we can count on. If something goes wrong, we need you to protect all the visitors."

Fred puffed out his chest. "Me?"

"The one and only." Mon-El clapped the security guard on the shoulder.

A second later, the one and only Fred had a twin.

Supergirl cringed. "Mon-El, your new power . . ."

The Daxamite glanced down at the security uniform he was now wearing. "I can totally explain this," he told an openmouthed Fred.

"Don't bother," Fred said in a faint voice, backing away. "I'll go . . . uh . . . clear the rooms."

"Can you point us toward the sunken treasure exhibit before you go?" asked Supergirl.

The security guard pulled a map from his back pocket. "Take this hall all the way to the end and turn left." He fixed her with pleading eyes. "And try not to break anything."

"Alex?" Supergirl spoke into her comm as Fred jogged away. "Mon-El and I are going to move in on Dr. Wanabi."

"OK," her sister said. "We're almost there. Be careful!"

Supergirl smirked at Mon-El's security guard guise. "Do you want to charge in like that, or turn into yourself first?"

"I'd love to be me, but I don't know how." Mon-El rubbed his neck. "Unless you want to knock me out. That seems to work."

"Let's save that for when you deserve it," teased Supergirl. "Yesterday when you changed into me, you said you wanted to connect with me. Can you try connecting with yourself?"

"I guess." Mon-El frowned and placed a hand on his own shoulder.

Supergirl snickered. "Not like that. Connect with who you are on the *inside*." She placed her hands on both sides of his face. "Close your eyes."

Mon-El did as she instructed. "Shouldn't we be chanting and burning incense for this?"

"Shh." She released him. "Think about everything that makes you who you are. Your sense of humor and your bravery and how good you are with people."

"Let's forget Dr. Wanabi," said Mon-El. "We can just stay here, and you can keep saying nice things about me." He smiled at Supergirl and opened his eyes.

Eyes she recognized.

"It's working!" she cheered. "Keep going."

Mon-El closed his eyes again, and soon all his features replaced Fred's.

"Welcome back," Supergirl told him, planting a kiss on his nose. "Now let's go save the day!"

She and Mon-El sped past various exhibits until they reached the end of the hall. Just past the left turn, they spotted Dr. Wanabi sitting on a bench. Thankfully, the bars of orichalcum were still stacked inside a display case.

"Dr. Wanabi!" Supergirl approached him. "You're coming with us."

Dr. Wanabi gasped and jumped to his feet. "Supergirl!"

"That's right," she said with a smug smile. "Mon-El, grab the orichalcum while I have a little chat with Dr. Wanabi."

Mon-El didn't move. "With my bare hands? After what it did to you?"

Supergirl swiveled her head to look at him. "If you're worried, then use your jacket," she whispered.

"Sure," he said. Then hesitated. "Except, I just bought it. What if—"

"Mon-El!" she said in a sharper voice.

"Right," he said, hurrying forward. "OK." He reached toward the display case, then thought better of it and squatted beside it. "Sorry, Fred." Wrapping his arms around the base of the display, Mon-El ripped the whole thing from the floor.

Supergirl winced but grabbed Dr. Wanabi's arm. "We're going on a little trip."

Dr. Wanabi shook his head. "You should leave if you don't want to get hurt. I've got people coming to help me."

"Yeah? Well, so do we," said Supergirl.

Suddenly, she heard the snap of a whip and felt a sharp sting at her waist. Supergirl glanced down and saw what appeared to be a thick blond braid wrapped around her middle.

"What the—"

The braid tightened, jerking Supergirl backward into Mon-El, who tumbled over and dropped the display stand. The glass case shattered when it hit the floor, and the orichalcum bars spilled out with metallic clunks.

Mon-El peeled off his jacket and tossed it over the orichalcum bars, scooping them up just as a blast of fire shot in front of him. With a yelp, he leaped back into a slimy ooze, losing all traction beneath his feet. Mon-El slipped and skidded, fighting to stay upright, while a man in green swim trunks slid past him through the slime.

"Thanks for wrapping my to-go order!" the man said, hefting the contents of Mon-El's jacket under one arm.

"Hey! Put that down!" Mon-El shouted, skittering toward him.

"Honey, would you do the honors?" The man in the swim trunks nodded to a woman holding a ball of flame.

Mon-El's eyes widened. "Uh-oh."

Across the room, Supergirl struggled with several braids that had lashed around each of her limbs. The little girl who owned them cackled with glee.

"I really hate to do this," Supergirl told her, "but it's time for you to get a haircut."

She squinted at each braid, singeing it off with a blast from her heat vision.

The girl screamed and dropped to her knees, gathering up her fallen locks.

Supergirl ran toward Mon-El to help him, but something grabbed one of her ankles and tripped her. Supergirl turned and saw a hand jutting out from a portal in the floor. Then another hand appeared and a man began to pull himself up, using Supergirl as an anchor. She zapped him with her heat vision, but the man's skin simply absorbed the blast.

"Oh, that can't be good," she murmured.

The man's weight pulled at her leg, causing her to slide toward the portal. Supergirl lay flat on her stomach and shot several holes in the floor with her heat vision, using the holes as handholds.

"Mon-El!" she shouted. "We're about to have more company!"

"Great!" he shouted back, ducking a fireball. "I could use a fair fight!"

The man climbing through the portal finally emerged and released Supergirl. While he was still on his hands and knees, Supergirl rolled onto her back and kicked him hard in one shoulder.

The man grinned but didn't budge. It was as if he were absorbing all her attacks, like a human sponge.

Supergirl scrambled to her feet and charged toward Mon-El's fiery attacker.

"Don't worry about me! Stop Mr. Slick over there!" Mon-El pointed to the man in swim trunks who was skating down the hall on slime-covered feet, carrying Mon-El's orichalcum-filled jacket.

Supergirl flew after the man and tackled him, but he wriggled free and skated off with a backward glance and a laugh.

"Guess I'm the one that got away!" crowed Mr. Slick.

Alex stepped in his path holding a harpoon gun. "Wanna bet?"

She pulled the trigger and a massive net shot from the gun, entangling Mr. Slick. He struggled to free himself, but magnetic weights at the net's edges clamped firmly to one another and to the orichalcum.

Supergirl landed by her sister while DEO agents ran past them into the fray. "That was amazing! How did you know to bring that?" She gestured to the harpoon gun.

"After J'onn talked with you about repercussions, he and Winn researched the residents of Shady Oaks, trying to think of powers they might develop." Alex nodded to the net. "That was actually meant for a fishmonger." She stopped two DEO agents and pointed out Mr. Slick. "Jackson, Whitby, take this man and what he's carrying to the van."

"You got it," one of them said.

Alex looked at Supergirl. "Shall we?" She nodded toward the commotion in the next room.

"Not without me," said a deep voice muffled by metal and mask. Guardian appeared beside them, and the trio ran toward the exhibit room, where the chaos had tripled in Supergirl's absence.

Mon-El and six DEO agents were battling a dozen super-citizens while Dr. Wanabi cowered in the corner. The woman with the fireballs was in handcuffs, and Mon-El was now wrestling the Human Sponge. Supergirl raced across the room to help, and Alex started to follow—until an oversized marionette leaped onto her back, waving a broken piece of glass. With a swipe of his shield, Guardian sent the puppet flying.

Alex gawked at it. "Looks like I've got my nightmare lined up for tonight."

"Where did all these people come from?" Guardian asked, sidestepping a man with horns.

"There's . . . a . . . portal!" Supergirl said, freeing herself from a headlock. "We have to disrupt it! Winn?"

"Let me think, let me think!" his voice answered in her ear. "Oh! Have any objects come through the portal alone? Like a gun or a knife . . . something not carbon-based?"

"Does Pinocchio's evil twin count?" asked Alex.

"That's Stringleshanks!" the marionette screeched, lunging for her again.

Alex ducked, and the marionette went hurtling past.

"As disturbing as it sounds, chances are that's a real person," said Winn. "Whoever created the portal probably can't transport just nonliving things, so tossing in a vase or something should do the trick."

"Let's hope so!" Supergirl picked up the pedestal Mon-El had ripped from the floor and hurled it at the portal. As the stone pedestal passed through, the edges of the portal fizzled. A second later, the portal disappeared, leaving the pedestal half-wedged in the floor.

The disappearance of their escape route seemed to spook the supercitizens. They stopped attacking and started running for the exits.

Several of the DEO agents cheered, and one shouted, "We beat 'em!"

Alex frowned and grabbed him by the arm. "Jackson! What are you doing here?"

Jackson glanced at her in confusion. "Ma'am?"

Alex pointed toward the exit. "I told you and Whitby to wait at the van!"

The other DEO agent just stared. "Ma'am, I've been in here since we arrived."

Alex froze. "What?"

Supergirl approached her sister. "What's going on?"

Alex tapped her earpiece. "Whitby, status report."

No response.

"Whitby, do you copy?" Alex ran from the room.

"Alex! Talk to me!" Supergirl flew after her.

"I had Jackson and Whitby take that supercitizen we caught to the van," Alex said between breaths, "but Jackson's been inside the whole time. So unless he can be in two places at once . . ."

Supergirl's jaw tightened. "Whitby's with two of the evil supercitizens."

She surged ahead and out the front doors to the DEO van. Whitby lay unconscious on the ground next to a pile of shredded netting.

Mr. Slick and the Jackson impostor were gone.

And so was all the orichalcum.

# 11

ONCE, WHEN MON-EL WAS A BOY, A servant's son had dared him to climb to the palace roof. Mon-El made it only ten feet or so before he lost his footing and fell, striking his head on the wall.

That skull-throbbing pain was exactly what he felt now.

He, Supergirl, and Alex were back at the DEO being debriefed by J'onn after their disastrous attempt at recovering the orichalcum. After Supergirl discovered it gone, she'd scoured the area for the supercitizens, but they'd vanished without a trace, leaving their captured friends (the horned Hard Charger and fiery Flamethrower) behind.

Luckily, Supergirl and Alex were both slouching in their chairs, disappointed, so he could hide his headache by burying his head in his hands and mirroring their sentiment.

"The strike team did as directed," Alex told J'onn. "It's my fault for not paying more attention."

Supergirl squinted at her sister. "You're not a screwup, Alex."

Mon-El sucked in his breath and sat up straighter, despite the pain. Where had *that* comment come from?

"What? I never said I was." The color rose in Alex's cheeks.

"No, but you're thinking it," Supergirl said sagely.

Mon-El frowned. How could she know what Alex was thinking?

"And you're wrong," Supergirl continued. "You're brilliant and tough as nails and—"

Alex didn't seem cheered by her sister's pep talk, but Supergirl appeared to be oblivious, continuing to rattle off Alex's best qualities.

"I'm sorry I let such a huge mistake happen on my watch." Alex turned her attention back to the DEO director.

Supergirl tugged at Alex's sleeve. "You're not listening. You didn't make a—"

"Yes, I did, Kara!" Alex whirled on her sister. "And talking about how great I am just reminds me that I shouldn't have let this happen."

Supergirl held up her hands. "Jeez, sorrrry. I thought you could use a pick-me-up."

Mon-El leaned toward Supergirl and whispered, "I'm gonna guess that's *not* what she wants."

Alex grunted in exasperation and faced J'onn once more. He regarded Alex with a stern but fatherly expression.

"A mistake was made," J'onn said, "but we learn from it and improve our tactics. Correct, Agent Danvers?"

Alex's shoulders relaxed a little, but she nodded curtly. "Yes, sir. It won't happen again."

"I know it won't," said J'onn with a tight smile. "Now, Mr. Schott, any progress on tracking down the orichalcum or our nefarious friends?" J'onn turned to Winn.

"Nada," said Winn, frowning at his screen. "Whoever's creating portals for them is *really* good. I haven't found a single trace of virtual particles."

"We have to steal that orichalcum back," said Supergirl, getting to her feet. "Now that they have all that potential power *and* Dr. Wanabi—"

"Actually, they don't," said a familiar voice.

Mon-El and the others turned to see Guardian walking down the control room steps, pushing a bedraggled Dr. Wanabi before him.

"I found him hiding in a coffin at the museum," said Guardian.

"Oh, when I'm finished with him, he's gonna need a coffin all right," growled Supergirl, storming toward the scientist.

"Wait." Mon-El leaped out of his chair and grasped Supergirl's hand, using it to steady himself for a second. "Let's see what he can tell us first."

Supergirl faced Mon-El. "This whole mess is because . . ." She trailed off and her forehead wrinkled. "Are you OK?"

Mon-El stood as tall as he could. "Yeah, I'm fine," he said, even as the edges of his vision darkened. "Why do you ask?"

"You don't look very good." She placed a hand to his forehead. "And you're burning up."

"I feel fine," he repeated, closing his eyes and focusing on a connection with Supergirl. When he opened his eyes, he caught his reflection—or rather *her* reflection—in a monitor. "Do I look better now?"

"Not really." Winn pointed at his face. "Now your nose is bleeding. Like your greatest weakness is low humidity."

"What?" Mon-El wobbled on the spot, and Supergirl reached out to steady him.

Behind them, there was a clatter and thud.

"James!" Alex rushed over to where he'd collapsed on the floor. She pulled off his helmet to reveal blood spilling from *his* nose as well.

Dr. Wanabi stood frozen in place, watching in horror as Alex pried James's eyes open and studied his pupils. "Not again," Dr. Wanabi whispered.

"You've seen this before?" Supergirl asked, letting go of Mon-El long enough to grab him a box of tissues.

"Of course he has," muttered Alex. "It's happening to all the supercitizens, isn't it?"

Dr. Wanabi swallowed hard and nodded.

J'onn pointed at Winn. "Mr. Schott, have the infirmary prep two cots for Mr. Olsen and Super . . . uh . . . Mon-El," he corrected himself.

"Already on it," said Winn, a phone to one ear.

Mon-El shook his head, blond hair bouncing, as he blotted his nose with a tissue. "I'm fine. I don't need the infirmary."

"Mon-El, you may heal faster than James, but you've still got orichalcum in your veins," said Supergirl.

"So do you," he shot back.

She smiled bitterly. "Yeah, but my collapse isn't scheduled until tomorrow." She glanced at Dr. Wanabi. "That's right, isn't it? The poison doesn't hit you for about twenty-four hours?"

Dr. Wanabi frowned. "No, it doesn't work that way. It spreads faster the more people use their powers."

"The cots are ready." Winn pointed down the hall.

Supergirl ducked under one of Mon-El's arms while J'onn hoisted James over one shoulder. Dr. Wanabi stayed rooted to the spot until Alex snapped a pair of handcuffs on him.

"You're coming with us," she said. "You've got a lot to answer for."

Supergirl staggered to the infirmary with Mon-El while J'onn walked behind them, carrying James. Alex followed, escorting Dr. Wanabi, and Winn brought up the rear.

"This is different," said Dr. Hoshi while Supergirl helped Mon-El onto a cot. "Two Supergirls."

"I was trying to prove I was healthy," said Mon-El.

Dr. Hoshi shrugged. "Hey, I don't judge . . ."

She dragged a special sunlamp over to Mon-El and flipped it on, soaking him with intense solar waves.

"Let there be light!" she said.

Within moments, the throbbing in Mon-El's head lessened.

"Your nose stopped bleeding," said Supergirl with a sigh of relief.

"Now for the real test," said Mon-El.

He closed his eyes and focused on connecting with his true self. His scalp began to itch as his hair shrank to its normal length, and the pressure of wearing Supergirl's costume eased as he felt his own clothes return. The best part was that he didn't feel any worse for it.

Mon-El opened his eyes and saw Supergirl smiling.

"You're getting better at that," she said.

Mon-El glanced at James, who was struggling to keep

his eyes open. He, unfortunately, didn't get the same healing benefit from the sun.

"Don't look so worried," Dr. Hoshi told Mon-El as she hooked James up to an IV. "I've got a few tricks up my sleeve."

"What's in here?" Alex thumped the IV bag. "Saline?"

"EDTA," said Dr. Hoshi. "For chelation."

"EDTA? Chelation?" Supergirl shook her head in confusion.

Before Dr. Hoshi could answer, Dr. Wanabi chimed in.

"EDTA's a synthetic amino acid," he said. "So it can bond with other molecules. Chelation will basically drag whatever the EDTA bonds with out of the body. I'm guessing orichalcum, in this case." He gave Dr. Hoshi a questioning look, and she smiled at him.

"That's right. I figured I'd try it since it works for lead poisoning," she said.

Alex nodded. "It's worth a shot."

"But won't that mean James loses his powers?" asked Winn.

Supergirl gave him an incredulous look. "Would you rather he be like this?" She gestured to their semiconscious friend.

Winn brushed a hand over the top of his hair. "No, but he's probably gonna freak. He's always wanted powers."

"Well, if this doesn't work, he may just get to keep them," said Dr. Hoshi.

Alex turned to Dr. Wanabi. "You're a scientist. And you were probably a decent person at one point. So why mess with an unknown substance in a building full of people? What were you thinking?"

Dr. Wanabi took a deep breath and wriggled in his hand-cuffs. "I was thinking of my sister. She has cancer, and I was hoping the orichalcum would help."

Alex blinked at him. "By killing her quicker?"

"Alex!" Supergirl smacked her arm. "The man's sister has cancer."

J'onn lifted a hand to halt the sisters' argument. "How did you think it could help, Dr. Wanabi?"

He settled onto a chair next to James. "I like to dive in my spare time, and among divers there are always myths and legends: mermaids, sirens, the lost city of Atlantis."

"Oh, that last one's actually a real thing," said Winn.

Dr. Wanabi nodded. "At first I didn't believe it, but a friend told me about a man who had failing kidneys and weeks to live. He went for a dive and"—Dr. Wanabi clapped his hands together, and everyone jumped—"his kidneys were healed."

"Let me guess," said Alex. "He happened to be diving near Atlantis."

Dr. Wanabi held up a finger. "My friend and I visited a different dive site nearby and heard *another* story. This one was about a woman who hoped to find enough treasure to pay off her debt. She went for a dive and a week later had all the money she needed."

J'onn leaned back against a counter. "The orichalcum was leaching into the water. The divers weren't getting what they wanted; they were getting powers that gave them what they wanted."

"Yes," said Dr. Wanabi. "But I didn't know that. I figured they'd found a"—he flexed his fingers, as if plucking the words from the air—"magic lamp or wishing coin." He sighed and rubbed his forehead. "I know that sounds ridiculous."

Supergirl snorted. "A magical imp once tried to make me his bride. Trust me. We get a lot of ridiculous around here."

"So, Dr. Wanabi, you and your friend decided to search for Atlantis?" prompted J'onn.

"Yes," said Dr. Wanabi, "but we needed money for the expedition, so we partnered with a diving company that provides exhibits to museums."

"Sea Kings," supplied Winn.

Dr. Wanabi looked taken aback. "Yes! You are good."

Winn shrugged and grinned. "I have a very particular set of skills."

"With funding from Sea Kings," Dr. Wanabi continued, "we bought sonar equipment to find Atlantis *and* special dive equipment to explore the entire city, including a vault of treasures."

Supergirl leaned forward. "The entire city? I'm surprised nobody stopped you."

Dr. Wanabi stared at her. "What are you talking about? Nobody lives down there."

Supergirl chuckled. "Sure they do. We've got a guyyy"— Alex cleared her throat and shook her head—"who, uh, thinks they do. Hector . . . in Accounting," Supergirl finished with a weak laugh.

"Well, he's wrong," said Dr. Wanabi. "Anyway, most of the treasure seemed ordinary. But when I picked up an orichalcum bar, even with my gloves on, I knew it was something different."

Alex crossed her arms. "So you saved some for yourself before turning the treasure over to the diving company."

"A small piece," said Dr. Wanabi, placing his index finger and thumb close together. "Just enough to see if it could help my sister."

Mon-El propped himself up on his elbows. "But you didn't help her. You tried to replicate the orichalcum. We found your notebook."

Dr. Wanabi jumped to his feet. "You have my notebook?"

J'onn pushed him back into his chair. "Yes, and you're not getting it back."

Dr. Wanabi struggled against him. "Please! I was working on my sister's cure. One that could help many!"

Supergirl picked up the notebook J'onn had left on the table the night before. Flipping through it, she frowned. "You mean the one with 'Sakura's Formula' written across the top and absolutely nothing underneath?" She turned the notebook so everyone could see.

Mon-El squinted at the Japanese characters and then at Supergirl. "You can read that?"

"You can't?" she glanced at the book. "Hey!" She smiled broadly. "I guess I understand Japanese now, too."

Dr. Wanabi snatched the notebook from Supergirl before anyone could stop him. "I was about to start work on the cure! I just needed a little more power."

Alex exchanged a look with J'onn. "You've been using the orichalcum on yourself?"

"Your superpower is enhanced intelligence," said J'onn, a look of understanding crossing his features.

"Yes." Dr. Wanabi glanced up. "But I'm still not smart enough to cure Sakura's cancer! I need more orichalcum!"

Supergirl knelt beside him. "Look at what it's done to my friend." She pointed at James. "I don't know how much is already in your system, but it's poison, and more might kill you."

"And cancer will kill my sister." Dr. Wanabi's lower lip trembled. "I have to find the cure," he whispered.

Supergirl took his hand. "Not like this."

Dr. Hoshi approached the team, and everyone shifted their attention.

"How is Mr. Olsen?" J'onn asked, though the expression on the woman's face didn't bode well.

"The chelation didn't work," she said, "but he's in stable condition now. His body must be fighting the orichalcum."

"That's good, right?" asked Supergirl.

Dr. Hoshi tilted her hand from side to side. "I've never worked with this substance before, so I can't guarantee Mr. Olsen won't relapse." She clucked her tongue. "I think the same will be true for other people who've been exposed."

Supergirl nodded and gripped Dr. Wanabi's hand tighter. "If you can't help your sister right now, can you at least help the other people of this city?" she asked him. "We need an antidote for the orichalcum."

Dr. Wanabi wiped at his eyes. "Y-yes. I think I can do it."

"Agent Danvers, uncuff our visitor," said J'onn. He bent close to Dr. Wanabi. "I trust you're a good man, but hurt my people, and I'll end you."

Dr. Wanabi swallowed hard but extended his cuffed hands. "I'll need a work space and a sample of the orichalcum, if you have it."

Winn stepped forward and passed him the tiny jar. "Right here."

"We have a lab you can use," Alex told Dr. Wanabi. "I've got a background in bioengineering, so I can help." She gestured to him, and he got to his feet.

"I'll take any you can give," said Dr. Wanabi, following her out of the infirmary.

"And I'll go back to searching for our little legion of doom," said Winn.

J'onn put a hand on his shoulder. "Check recent hospital and clinic admissions for bloody noses and fainting spells. The one upside I see to all this"—J'onn gestured around the infirmary—"is that our troublemaking supercitizens might be under the weather as well."

"You got it," Winn said, walking out.

"Maybe we'll have a quiet afternoon," Supergirl said hopefully.

J'onn smirked at her. "When have we ever had a quiet afternoon? I'll need you to be on hand if we call." He looked at Mon-El. "And you, too, if you're up for it."

"Of course," Mon-El said. "I feel way better." This time he wasn't lying.

"Glad to hear it from at least one of you." J'onn gave James one last glance before leaving the infirmary.

With everyone else gone or unconscious, Supergirl approached Mon-El with a winsome expression. "You had me a little worried there!"

She said it teasingly as she pinched his side, but he saw her eyebrows knit together for a split second.

Mon-El reached for her hand. "You don't ever have to worry about me, Kara. I'll always be here. Promise."

Supergirl's smile softened. "Good. I'll be back after I talk to Pryll."

She blew Mon-El a kiss and exited with a twirl.

He grinned and lay back to absorb some more sunlight.

Until something clamped around his arm.

Mon-El jumped and looked down at James, who gaped at him through wide eyes.

"Please," he whispered. "Don't let them take my powers."

## 12

**Y**OU DID NOT RETRIEVE THE orichalcum," Pryll said when Supergirl entered his cell. A new water-filled tank had replaced the broken one, but he was pacing the room instead of swimming.

"Do I look *that* guilty?" She sauntered over to him, hands clasped in front of her. "We're still working on it," she promised. "Some new enemies caught us by surprise."

Pryll frowned and stopped his pacing. "You should have let me assist. It is my duty."

Supergirl nodded. "To guard the treasures of Atlantis. I know." She remembered Dr. Wanabi's comment about the empty-looking city. "But you can't be the only one down there. Where are the other Atlanteans?" she finally asked.

Pryll stared at Supergirl for a moment and then lifted his chin. "I am charged with guarding the city's treasure, not its inhabitants. Where they are is not my concern."

"What about your family?" Supergirl tried again.

Pryll clenched his jaw but said nothing.

It was time for a different approach.

"I don't know if you knew this about me, but I'm an alien," said Supergirl. She settled on the floor and leaned back against Pryll's tank. "From a galaxy far, far away."

Pryll glanced down at her. "Where is *your* family?"

"Dead." She sighed. "The whole planet was destroyed."

Pryll crouched beside her. "I am sorry for you. How did you escape?"

"My parents sent me in a spaceship to follow my cousin here."

"Ah. So you have one family member at least," said Pryll. He gazed at the floor. "I watched my wife, Eleni, die during Atlantis's destruction. And my son, Jerro, who was patrolling our borders, never came home."

"Then *I* am sorry for *you* as well," said Supergirl.

"Atlantis is all I have left," Pryll continued. "Without it, my life has no purpose."

Supergirl gave him a small smile. "We'll get the orichalcum back. We've got everyone looking for it."

Pryll leaned forward, wide-eyed. "Everyone in your city? I am touched they would do this."

"Not everyone in the city," Supergirl said with a chuckle. "Everyone at the DEO!"

She stopped laughing as an idea struck her. "Wait a minute. Why *not* everyone in the city? Pryll, that's brilliant!" Supergirl scrambled to her feet. "I'll be back later."

"Supergirl!" Pryll called after her, but she'd already opened the door and zipped down the hall.

She skidded to a stop outside the infirmary. Mon-El was talking to James, who'd finally regained full consciousness.

"You're awake!" Supergirl approached James's cot. "How do you feel?"

James and Mon-El both jumped at her presence, and James smiled weakly.

"Like I just lost a tag team boxing match against Muhammed Ali, Mike Tyson, and, well, you," said James. "But I'm getting back to normal, slowly."

Supergirl glanced at Mon-El, who appeared stone-faced.

"Sorry, did I interrupt something?" she asked.

"Nope!" Mon-El forced a smile. "Just filling him in on what happened with Dr. Wanabi."

Supergirl put a hand on James's shoulder. "Thanks for finding him. We've got him working with Alex on an antidote to the orichalcum."

"That's what I hear," said James, glancing at Mon-El.

Supergirl wrung her hands together and winced. "And I know you've just been through a near-death experience, but I have a favor to ask. A CatCo-related favor."

James raised an eyebrow. "I'm listening."

"Tons of people reacted to my message about the super-citizens." She looked from James to Mon-El. "What if we could get that many people to react to a different message?"

"What do you mean?" asked Mon-El.

"Right now, we've got a building full of people looking for the evil supercitizens and the orichalcum," said Supergirl, gesturing around her. "But we could have *all* of National City looking. No confrontations, just information."

James leaned on one elbow. "A citywide stakeout? That's not a bad idea."

Mon-El raised a hand. "OK, but if someone *has* information, how do they let you know? Shine a light in the sky?"

Supergirl snickered. "That seems like overkill. They can just use the phone. We'll set up a hotline here at the DEO."

"Sounds like you've got this all figured out," said James. "So what do you need me for?"

Supergirl's cheeks warmed and she ducked her head. "Could you, um, record the message? I don't think anybody wants to hear from Supergirl right now."

James grinned and nodded. "Of course. Give me a few

minutes, and I'll go with you to the office." He snapped his fingers. "Hey, if we hurry, we could also post something in the evening issue of the *Tribune*."

The mention of the newspaper triggered a memory in Supergirl's mind. Snapper had written an op-ed piece for the *Tribune*—something that might explain why the mayor was upset. A visit to the *Tribune*'s floor at CatCo would be the perfect chance to check its archives.

"Great!" said Supergirl. "Meet me in the control room. I'm going to tell J'onn and Winn our idea."

She practically skipped down the hallway. Things were finally starting to come together.

"Kara!" Mon-El trotted after her. "Can I talk to you for a second?"

"Of course." She stopped to face him. "Is everything OK? You looked upset earlier."

"I'm fine," he said, waving away her concern. "I was just thinking . . ." He chewed his lip and smiled. "You know what? Never mind."

"Mon-El." Supergirl grabbed his hand. "What is it?"

He rubbed the back of his neck. "It's about that antidote Dr. Wanabi and Alex are working on. I think we should let people choose whether or not to take it."

Supergirl let go of Mon-El. That was the last thing she'd expected to hear him say. "But if people don't take the antidote, the orichalcum will keep making them sick."

"Yeah, but maybe people are OK with being sick if it means they get to keep their powers," he said with a shrug.

Supergirl wrinkled her forehead. "But we don't know if they get to keep their powers. We *do* know even trace amounts of orichalcum can be dangerous." She pointed down the hall to the infirmary.

"But not *too* dangerous, right?" asked Mon-El. "I mean, look at me. I'm fine."

Supergirl smirked at him. "You're also from a different planet and draw healing power from the sun."

"And James is doing better, too," Mon-El pointed out.

"I suppose," Supergirl said with a frown. "Are you bringing this up for the supercitizens . . . or for you?"

"Huh?" Mon-El blinked at her. "For them, of course. I couldn't care less."

But his eyes averted her gaze for a fraction of a second, and she heard an echo of his voice.

*This is important to me, Kara.*

Supergirl sighed. "Mon-El, we can't say it's OK for you to keep your new power but expect everyone else to give theirs up."

He shook his head. "I'm not saying that, Kara. I'm saying we should give people a choice."

"When one of those choices is to intentionally hurt themselves?" Supergirl crossed her arms. "Not on my watch."

Mon-El pressed his lips together and breathed through his nostrils. "You know, you've been making a lot of decisions for other people the last few days."

"Because they can't make good decisions for themselves!" Supergirl threw her hands in the air. "And now you're trying to put them in danger so you can keep your new power, which is even worse."

"So I'm the bad guy now?" Mon-El gave a mirthless chuckle. "Wow. I'd expect that kind of attitude from one of *my* people, but from you?" He turned on his heel and walked away.

"Mon-El!" Supergirl clenched her fists at her sides, but didn't go after him. He was obviously standing as firm on the issue as she was, and she had other things to worry about.

But she couldn't deny that it stung, just a little, to be compared to a Daxamite.

It took some convincing from both Supergirl and James, but J'onn finally agreed to their plan, insisting that he write the script for James's speech.

"Do not deviate from this." J'onn handed copies to James and Supergirl.

Supergirl read the script and glanced at Winn. "Call 1-800-BADDIES? That's the number you got?"

He made a face. "I wanted 1-800-BAD-GUYS, but the number keys were already being used by 1-800-ACE-GUYS, and their poker table sales are really taking off," he said.

James pocketed the script and nodded to Supergirl. "You ready?"

"Almost." She zipped around the corner and then reappeared as Kara. "If we land on the CatCo roof, I can fly us there." She held an arm open to James, who groaned and stepped closer.

"I hate this part," he said, gripping her waist tightly.

"It'll be over before you know it," Kara said, lifting them both into the air. "Hold on to your lunch!"

Kara and James shot out of the DEO building and touched down on the CatCo roof a few seconds later.

"You get ready to broadcast, and I'll take a copy of this speech down to the *Tribune*," Kara told James while he caught his breath.

James gave her a thumbs-up, so Kara took the stairs to the floor below and hurried up to a redheaded woman eating a slice of cake.

"Vicki V! Just the woman I wanted to see." Kara smiled broadly at her and held up the script. "I have a favor to ask."

The woman's eyes flitted over J'onn's speech. "Is this for real?"

"It is. Can you get it on the front page of the evening edition?"

Vicki clucked her tongue. "I suppose I could sneak it in." She held up the slice of cake. "It's my last day. What're they going to do, fire me?"

"Oh, right! You're leaving us for that other paper." Kara pouted her lower lip. "Aw, we'll miss you."

"I wish I could say the same." Vicki leaned close. "Between you and me, this place was driving me batty." She took the paper from Kara. "I'll let you know once it's done."

"Thanks!" Kara swung her arms and stayed rooted to the floor. "Could I ask one more teeny-tiny favor?"

Vicki guarded her plate with a fork. "You can't have my cake."

Kara laughed. "No, I was just hoping you could point out the archives."

"Oh!" Vicki laughed, too. "We're all digital at the *Tribune*, but I can pull them up from my laptop." She motioned for Kara to follow. "Are you looking for any article in particular?"

"An op-ed piece that Snapper Carr did," supplied Kara, at which point Vicki wrinkled her nose.

"Ugh. He's your boss, isn't he? Poor you!" Her fingers hammered on the keyboard, and an article appeared on the screen: "Outside of a Dog" by Snapper Carr.

"That's the one," said Kara, reading the piece.

*Switching to a strictly digital format (as is the mayor's wont) favors the well-to-do who can afford e-readers over the lower class who can't. While some devices will be made available to the public, they won't be enough to accommodate all, and we return to the Middle Ages, where knowledge is a privilege, not a right. Well done, Mayor. Here's hoping the voters still have enough intelligence to skip your name on the ballot come election time.*

Kara gritted her teeth. Snapper had set her up for failure from the beginning! He'd trashed the mayor, knowing the man would never want to talk to CatCo again, and then assigned Kara the interview, leaving out how difficult he'd made her task.

But Kara had been in plenty of difficult situations and wasn't about to let this one stop her. It was time for another visit to City Hall.

"Can you e-mail that article to me?" she asked Vicki, providing her e-mail address.

"You got it," said Vicki. "Any other teeny-tiny favors?" she asked with a smirk.

"I'm all done," Kara said, crossing her heart. "Have fun at your new job, OK?" She hugged Vicki. "And stay out of trouble."

Vicki hugged her back. "We're reporters, Kara. We live for trouble."

Kara smiled to herself. She supposed the same was true of superheroes.

It was a much more confident Kara Danvers who strode up the steps of City Hall.

Once again, Ms. Binder the information clerk greeted her with a cheery smile. "Welcome to City Hall! How can I help you?"

Kara studied her for a moment, listening to the woman's words. *I probably can't help you, but it's polite to ask.*

Ms. Binder posed as someone official, but no matter what Kara said or did, the clerk had no real power.

Good.

"The mayor's office is on the second floor, right?" Kara pointed above them.

Ms. Binder's smile didn't slip an inch. "You'll need an appointment."

"Not to see his assistant," said Kara, striding toward the elevator.

"Miss?" The clerk's voice lost its cheer as Kara pressed the up button. "Miss, you can't—"

The elevator dinged and the doors opened. With a defiant glance at Ms. Binder, Kara stepped inside.

"Have a lovely day," she said, waving as the doors closed.

She smiled at her reflection in the elevator's brass panel as she pressed the button for the second floor. *One gatekeeper down, one to go*, she thought.

Kara steeled herself as the elevator doors opened again. She followed signs that led to an open rotunda outfitted with a massive mahogany desk. Behind the desk sat a young woman who looked annoyed to be alive. The nameplate on her desk read COURTNEY KEVALIER.

"Can I help you?" she asked Kara without a hint of a smile.

"I'd like to speak with the mayor," said Kara.

Courtney's desk phone rang, and she held up a finger while she answered it. "Mayor Lowell's office." She frowned. "Yes, I know there's a young woman on her way to see me. I'm looking at her now. Why did you even let her upstairs?"

Kara tried to focus on Courtney's words without being annoyed that they were about her.

Unlike Ms. Binder, there *was* authority in the assistant's voice, and no sense of self-importance. There was, however, concern. But not for herself.

"What would have happened if she'd made it to the mayor?" Courtney barked into the phone. "Don't let it happen again if you want to keep your job!" She hung up and returned her attention to Kara. "Why are you here?"

"To interview the mayor," Kara said. "My boss—"

"Oh, God." Courtney sneered. "You're with CatCo, aren't you? Well, the mayor's busy." She leaned back in her chair and crossed her arms.

"I don't believe that," said Kara. "I'm pretty sure he's just upset about an op-ed piece Snapper Carr wrote."

Courtney's face was a mask. "The mayor's busy," she repeated.

"Snapper attacked the mayor's digital library initiative," Kara continued. "And if I'm not mistaken, that's pretty important to Mayor Lowell." She chuckled. "I mean, it even made the City Hall calendar."

Courtney picked up the handset of her phone. "Would you like security to show you out, or can you find the exit on your own?" Her scowl was one of annoyance, but Kara caught the protectiveness in her voice.

This woman would do anything for the mayor.

Kara clasped her hands behind her back. "You know, Ms. Kevalier, silence can be more dangerous than the truth. If the mayor refuses to speak to a member of the press, people might think he's hiding something."

Courtney paused with her fingers over the keypad of her phone. "So that's your play? Threatening the mayor?"

Kara shook her head. "I'm not threatening. I'm telling you what will happen. My boss wants me to interview Mayor Lowell, and I have no problem filling a half-page space in CatCo magazine with the words 'Mayor Lowell declined to comment.'"

The mayor's assistant gripped the handset so tightly her knuckles whitened. After a moment, she returned the handset to its cradle and reached for her computer mouse.

A few clicks later, she cleared her throat and asked, "Would Thursday at one o'clock be OK?"

"That would be great," said Kara, making a note in her phone. "I will see you—and the mayor—then."

"Looking forward to it," said Courtney without a hint of enthusiasm.

Kara nodded and walked briskly away before the mayor's assistant could change her mind and call security.

When Kara reached the ground floor, she heard a sobbing hiccup that made her slow her steps and glance to the side.

At the information desk, Ms. Binder was wiping her eyes and shuffling the same stack of papers over and over.

Kara chewed her lip and approached the desk. "Ms. Binder?"

The information clerk blinked back tears and pasted on her perfect smile. "How can I help you?"

Kara rubbed her hands together. "I'm sorry I got you in trouble. I really needed to see the mayor."

Ms. Binder shook her head. "You were just doing your job. I should be doing mine better."

"Oh, no!" Kara reached out to the woman. "Please don't think that. I'm sure nobody could do this job better. I'm just . . . really desperate to impress my boss," she confessed.

Ms. Binder let out a weak laugh. "Oh, I've been there."

"Anyway, I'm sorry again. I hope you have a lovely day." Kara tapped the desk with her index finger. "I *do* mean that."

The clerk smiled at her, and this time it was genuine. "You, too, hon."

Kara resumed her stride but didn't walk as tall anymore.

She'd finally set up an interview with the mayor, but for some reason, it didn't feel like a victory at all.

# 13

ALEX HAD NEVER FELT MORE victorious. She and Dr. Wanabi were looking at a microscope slide they'd magnified and projected onto the wall. The slide contained red blood cells interspersed with scarlet-colored crystals of orichalcum. An hour earlier, white blood cells had been barraging the crystals, and the crystals had been twice the size.

"The white blood cells have finally stopped attacking the orichalcum," said Dr. Wanabi. "I can feel the difference in my body." He rubbed his arm where Alex had drawn blood.

Since Dr. Wanabi had been responsible for creating the supercitizens, he agreed to be the guinea pig for finding the antidote.

"It looks like the orichalcum in your blood is getting smaller, too," said Alex. "Did our antidote do that?"

Dr. Wanabi shook his head. "I used my enhanced mental powers to work out this formula, which used up a large portion of the orichalcum in my system."

"Huh." Alex rubbed her chin. "So the orichalcum will leave people's bodies once they've maxed out their powers. I mean, if it doesn't kill them first."

"Well, that's what our antidote is for," Dr. Wanabi reminded her. "To keep the supercitizens' immune systems from overreacting to the orichalcum."

"James will be happy to hear that," spoke a voice from the doorway. "Kara will not."

Alex and Dr. Wanabi turned around. Mon-El was leaning against the door frame, hands in his pockets and a troubled expression on his face.

Alex gave him a small smile. "She'll come around. Do you know if she and James got the broadcast out?"

Mon-El nodded. "It aired twenty minutes ago, and Winn's already been slammed with phone calls."

Alex's smile widened. "Even more good news!" She clapped Dr. Wanabi on the shoulder. "If you need me, I'll be in the control room," she said, hurrying into the hall. "Mon-El, you coming?"

"Uh . . . should someone stay with him?" asked Mon-El, hitching a thumb in Dr. Wanabi's direction.

"We used the last of our orichalcum to make the antidote," Alex said in a soft voice. "And I'm pretty sure his former friends would rather kill him than take him back. He'll be fine."

She cleared her throat as she approached Winn's computer, where he was talking with J'onn. "We've found a way to stop the side effects of the orichalcum, and it looks like it dissolves with use. What's *your* good news?" She pointed to Winn and J'onn.

"We don't have any yet," said J'onn.

Alex's eyebrows lifted. "What? But Mon-El just told me you got a ton of calls."

"Yeah." Winn scoffed and handed her a stack of papers. "Lots of winners."

Alex shuffled through the tips they'd received. "Supercitizen wants to help, supercitizen wants to help, man saw a bear with a picnic basket . . . ha ha ha." She held up a piece of paper. "What about this one? A woman saw a little girl walk into a mirror."

Winn blew a raspberry and made a thumbs-down gesture. "It wasn't a mirror; it was a doorway. The little girl had a twin sister, and they were dressed alike because they have cruel parents."

Alex snickered and kept reading the papers. "Man, there are a lot of supercitizens who want to help fight the bad guys once we find them."

"It's too bad none can actually lead us to them," said J'onn.

Alex tossed the papers on Winn's desk. "I take it your search of hospitals and clinics didn't turn anything up?"

"I'm pretty sure the evil supercitizens have someone with healing powers," said Winn. "There were at least two nurses living at Shady Oaks."

Alex sighed. "Well, it's still early. Someone's bound to spot something."

She felt her phone vibrate against her hip, and when she pulled it out, Maggie's name was on the screen.

"Oh no, I was supposed to meet Maggie for coffee!" She answered the phone and walked off the control room floor. "Hey, sweetie! I am *so* sorry, but we're still trying to track down those supercitizens who took the orichalcum."

"I thought something like that might have happened," said Maggie. "Is there anything I can do to help?"

"Only if you have a police dog trained to sniff out Atlantean metal," Alex said wryly. "We have no idea where these people are hiding."

"Hmm. Have you factored in distance decay?" Maggie asked.

"Uh . . . since I have no idea what that is, I'm going to say no," said Alex.

Maggie laughed. "The farther you get from something, the less likely you are to interact with it," she explained. "For cops, it means people don't tend to commit crimes far from home—"

"They commit them closer to home," Alex finished for her.

"Bingo," said Maggie.

"Sweetie, you are the *best*. When I'm done here, I'm bringing you the biggest slice of tiramisu you've ever seen." Alex hurried back to the control room.

Maggie laughed again. "Just remember this the next time NCPD needs a favor. But I will also take the tiramisu."

Alex ended the call and gripped the back of Winn's chair. "Can you map all the crimes committed since we quarantined Shady Oaks yesterday afternoon?"

"Absolutely," he said, pressing each key with a flourish.

"Something on your mind, Agent Danvers?" asked J'onn.

Alex watched the video wall as recent crimes began to appear on a map of National City. "Maggie thinks the evil supercitizens will be committing crimes close to their hideout. If we can find an area with an increase in crime since yesterday morning—"

"We can find our supercitizens," said J'onn. He turned his attention to the video wall, too.

"Looks like we've got a hot zone," said Winn. "Near the Theater District."

Alex shook her head. "There are hundreds of places to hide there."

Mon-El bent over Winn's computer. "Can you check the rooftops of the buildings?"

"Uh, sure," he said, zooming in on aerial footage. "What am I looking for?"

"Bee Breather had to keep his pets somewhere," said Mon-El. "They must have a hive."

"Clever." Winn pointed at him and grinned. "And I can do one better. Every warm-blooded creature puts off a heat signature, right?"

Mon-El gave him a dubious look. "You're going to look for a bee's heat signature?"

"I'm going to look for a *cluster* of them, since bees swarm in, well, swarms," said Winn. He tapped a few keys and gestured to the video wall. "And there we have it."

An aerial camera focused on the roof of a building that was accented with concrete angels on each corner. At the roof's center sat a large wooden beekeeper's box.

"The Imperial Theater," said J'onn.

"We've got 'em!" Alex shook her fist triumphantly. "Winn, assemble a—"

J'onn held up a hand. "Let's not rush into this situation

half-cocked, Agent Danvers. We don't know what kind—or even how many—supercitizens we're up against."

Winn changed his view of the building. "I count at least fifteen human heat signatures."

"And who knows if there are more roaming the streets," pointed out Mon-El.

Alex rubbed her forehead. "You're right. OK, what's our plan, then?" she asked J'onn.

"That, I haven't figured out yet," he admitted.

There was a whooshing sound behind them, and Kara appeared, phone pressed to one ear and a scowl on her face.

"She took it the wrong way!" Kara exclaimed into the mouthpiece. "Do I look like the kind of person who threatens people?" She held the phone away from her ear and stared at it in shock. "Well, you know what *you* look like?" Kara asked the person on the other end. "You . . . look like a guy who's about to be proven wrong!" She stamped her foot.

Alex shook her head. Snapper.

Kara listened to her boss speak for a moment, pressing her lips into a tighter and tighter line. "I will not apologize to Courtney Kevalier. I played her game to get the interview, and she's just upset she lost." Kara shook her head. "I won't do it. No, I won't. No, I—" Kara stared at her phone again and growled. "Yeah, you better hang up!"

"Hey, honey. How was work?" Mon-El intoned.

Alex sucked in her breath. Mon-El was already on Kara's bad list, so it probably wasn't a great idea to tease her.

Apparently, however, Kara was more upset at Snapper than at her boyfriend.

"Snapper is unbelievable," she told Mon-El. "Do you know why Mayor Lowell canceled my interview? Because Snapper, who arranged that interview by the way, trash-talked him. Snapper set me up to fail!"

Mon-El frowned. "Maybe Supergirl could talk to the mayor."

Kara shook her head. "I don't want to play that card. Besides, I managed to get the interview."

"That's great!" said Alex. "So why all the yelling?"

Kara rolled her eyes. "Because I just *lost* the interview. Apparently, Mayor Lowell's assistant told him I was dismissive and threatening and bullied my way into an interview."

J'onn crossed his arms. "What? That doesn't sound like you."

"No, it doesn't." Alex put an arm around Kara. "Dismissive? My little sister would never blow someone off."

"Exactly," said Kara. She cleared her throat. "Except I kind of did."

"What?" Alex glanced at her sister.

"I apologized after!" said Kara.

"So you might have been dismissive. But threatening?" Mon-El scoffed. "I'm sure you didn't say, 'If the mayor doesn't talk to me, it'll hurt his career.'" He chuckled, but stopped at the guilty expression on Kara's face. "Did you?"

She fiddled with her glasses. "Not in those exact words . . ." She grimaced and dropped into a chair. "Aww, man! I *did* threaten and bully."

Alex squeezed her shoulder. "I'm sure it's not that bad."

Kara gave her sister a look of disbelief. "The mayor called my boss, Alex."

"But you didn't get fired." Alex smiled hopefully.

Kara slumped in the chair. "How are things going here? Did you come up with an antidote?"

"Eh," said Alex, tilting her hand from side to side. "We can stop people's immune systems from attacking the orichalcum, but it won't be out of their bodies until they fully use it."

"That's . . ." Kara squinted. "Would that be considered good news? I mean, you get to keep your new power." She gestured at Mon-El, who frowned.

"I told you, I wasn't asking for myself," he said. "Since it doesn't really matter anymore, I might as well tell you. I was asking for James."

"James?" Kara bowed her head and chuckled ruefully. "Mon-El, I'm sorry. I misunderstood." She glanced up at him, her eyebrows slanted in sadness. "I'm really . . ." The rest of the sentence caught in her throat, and she got up without another word.

"Kara." Alex reached for her, but Kara raised her hands defensively and wriggled past.

"I'm gonna check on Pryll," she said.

She ducked her head again and made a beeline for the prison cells.

"Kara, wait." Mon-El chased after her, leaving Alex to exchange awkward glances with Winn and J'onn.

"How about that plan?" she asked, rubbing her palms together.

Kara could hear Mon-El calling her name, but she could also feel tears building in her eyes.

"Just give me a couple minutes, OK?" she said, taking off her glasses.

A burst of air hit her, and Mon-El was by her side.

"Crap, I forgot you could move so fast." She wiped at her eyes and pasted on a smile. "What's up?"

"Don't give me that." Mon-El took her hand. "Something's going on, and it's not just about you and me. What is it?"

Kara pocketed her glasses and glanced at the fading red mark on her hand—the hand that had absorbed the orichalcum. "I can speak Atlantean." She looked up at Mon-El. "I can read Japanese. I can hear the truth in people's words, even if they say something different."

Mon-El's forehead wrinkled. "Yeah, and that's been really helpful."

Kara exhaled sharply and leaned back against the wall. "But it hasn't. Pryll's upset even though I told him we'll find his treasure, the supercitizens hate Supergirl, my boss doesn't appreciate me, I couldn't get through to the security guard before the museum heist, I made Alex feel bad *after* the museum heist, I bullied two people at the mayor's office, and you and I started fighting about the orichalcum antidote." She paused for a breath. "I even accused you of making it about yourself when you weren't!"

Mon-El gave her a sympathetic smile. "Kara, we're going to argue. It's part of being a couple." He squinted. "I think. This is all new territory."

She rubbed her hand. "I thought this new power would help me communicate better, but everything still goes wrong." She shook her head. "I am *really* bad at understanding people."

"No." Mon-El gripped her shoulders. "Kara Zor-El, you are one of the most understanding creatures I know."

She let out a frustrated sigh. "Then why am I having so much trouble getting through to people?"

He shrugged. "Maybe you're not giving them what they want."

Kara's forehead wrinkled. "What do you mean?"

"Let's say I ask you for . . . ice cream," said Mon-El. "You understand that I want ice cream, but instead of bringing me mint chocolate chip, which is my favorite, you bring me Rocky Road, which is yours."

"But you never told me what you wanted," she argued. Then a thought struck her. "And I never asked. I chose for you." Kara bumped her head against the wall. "That's what I've been doing, isn't it? I'm giving people what *I* think they should have."

"It kinda sounds like it. Your ideas are here, and theirs are here." Mon-El held his hands a few inches apart. "As soon as you figure out what they really want . . ." He brought his hands together.

Kara nodded. It made perfect sense. She'd convinced Dr. Wanabi to create the antidote because he wanted to save lives. And she'd gotten through to the information clerk because Ms. Binder wanted to be noticed at work, just like Kara did.

Mon-El tugged Kara to a standing position and wrapped his arms around her. "You are more than just your powers,

Kara. You have a kind heart and a determined spirit and a clever mind. Even if you were human, you would still be a super girl."

Kara rolled her eyes but smiled. "You know, you can be pretty smart sometimes."

"So can you," he said. "That hotline idea was pretty clever."

"Oh yeah!" Kara backed away. "I forgot to ask. How's it working out?"

Mon-El made a face. "There are a lot of supercitizens who want to help, but none who can give us any leads. Luckily, we found the bad guys on our own."

Kara's eyes widened. "Why didn't you say something earlier? Let's go!"

She grabbed his hand, but he didn't move.

"J'onn wants us to have a plan first."

Kara scoffed. "A plan?" She paused. "Oh, wait. No, that's a good idea. Do we know what we're up against?"

Footsteps padded around the corner, and a moment later Alex appeared. "We'll find out soon enough. How do you feel about a recon mission after dark?"

"Perfect! That'll give me just enough time to write my superdrug article." Kara entwined her arms around one of Alex's and gave her sister an adoring look. "If you can call Maggie and ask her to be my credible NCPD source?"

Alex took her phone out of her pocket. "I'm going to have to take her to Italy for tiramisu," she muttered, dialing Maggie's number.

Kara smiled and kissed Alex's cheek and then Mon-El's. "Thank you! Let me know when Maggie gets here."

"What? Where are you going?" asked Mon-El.

"To talk to Winn and then Pryll," she said with a firm nod. "It's time I give him what he wants."

# 14

**Y**OU TOLD HIM WHAT?!" J'ONN roared, giving Kara an incredulous look.

A few hours had passed since she'd talked to Pryll, and the DEO team was now prepping for the recon mission. Kara figured it was a good time to bring up the conversation, since J'onn would be too distracted to get upset.

Apparently, she was wrong.

"I told Pryll he could help us retrieve the orichalcum when the time comes." Kara said, jutting out her chin and standing her ground, though J'onn now towered over her. "Don't worry. I have it all planned out."

Alex rubbed her forehead. "Kara, that wasn't your call to make."

"Maybe not, but it was the right one," Kara insisted, looking from J'onn to Alex. "All Pryll has wanted since he got here was to reclaim his treasure, not to wait around for someone else to do it. His pride is tied to this."

"His pride is a liability." J'onn crossed his arms. "Need I remind you that he threw you and your sister across the room while trying to escape?"

Kara opened her mouth to protest again, but Mon-El stepped forward. "I agree with Kara. Pryll should be involved. He's the last of his kind."

"So am I," said J'onn.

"Then you can understand," said Kara, grabbing J'onn's arm. "What if you were charged with protecting a Martian artifact, and it was stolen? Wouldn't you want to be the one to recover it?"

J'onn was silent for a moment. Then he pointed at Kara. "No more decisions without my consent." He walked over to Winn's computer. "Mr. Schott, have you finished Mon-El's voice modulator?"

Since the DEO had captured Hard Charger and Flamethrower, J'onn, who could shape-shift on his own, and Mon-El, who could shape-shift with his new power, planned to impersonate them and infiltrate the supercitizen hideout. And since Kara hadn't been seen by the evil supercitizens in her human guise, she'd be joining them, with Alex and Winn watching remotely.

"One new voice, made to order," Winn said, handing a tiny metal disk to Mon-El. "Just peel off the backing and stick it to your throat." Winn tapped his own Adam's apple.

"Won't that be a little obvious?" asked Alex as Mon-El attached the disk. The shiny metal reflected the lights of the control room.

"When Mon-El changes into Hard Charger, the disk should disappear, along with Mon-El's usual appearance," said J'onn. To prove his point, he shifted into the guise of Flamethrower. Any semblance of J'onn vanished.

Alex spoke into an intercom. "Bring Prisoner 60 to the control room."

"How does this work?" Mon-El pointed to the voice modulator.

"Press it once to turn it on, and again to turn it off," said Winn.

Mon-El pressed the disk and asked, "How do I sound?" in a harsh, nasal voice.

"Obnoxious and perfect," said Winn. He handed plastic tubes of liquid to J'onn, Mon-El, and Kara. "These contain micro-cams so Alex and I can see what you see. You put them in like contact lenses."

Kara unscrewed her tube and fished out the micro-cam. The circle resembling the iris was blue like hers, except for a few intricate copper traces running through it. She pressed the micro-cam against her eye and blinked a few times to fix it in place. "How's that?" she asked Winn.

He turned toward his computer and punched a few keys. A side-angle view of him at his computer appeared on-screen, with KARA written across the top. The picture went black for a moment as Kara blinked.

"Perfect," said Winn. He punched a few more keys to check J'onn's and Mon-El's micro-cams just as two DEO agents appeared with a scowling Hard Charger between them.

Hard Charger's scowl turned into a look of confusion at the sight of Flamethrower hanging out with her captors.

"Elaine? What are you doing out here?" he asked J'onn.

"Showtime," Mon-El whispered to Kara. He reached out and put a hand on Hard Charger's shoulder. "Hey, buddy," he said in a soothing voice. "I'll bet you're pretty confused right now."

"I thought she was a Dominant like me. But now . . ." He trailed off, and his eyes widened as Mon-El shifted to match his appearance.

"Surprise!" Mon-El threw his arms open, and Hard Charger gasped. "You see this in the mirror every day," Mon-El told him. "I don't know why it scares you now."

Hard Charger backed away from Mon-El and into J'onn, who grabbed one of his arms.

"You referred to me as a Dominant. Is that what the residents of Shady Oaks call themselves?" he asked.

Hard Charger swallowed and nodded. "Those of us who stayed together, anyway. The ones with more dominant powers."

"Charming," said Alex. She nodded to the DEO agents. "You can take him back now."

"No, wait!" cried Hard Charger. "I can give you information! I can tell you where our hideout is!" Horns sprouted from his head, and he tried to head-butt one of the DEO agents, but the other one clubbed him with a baton.

"Man, he caved quick," Kara said, watching the DEO agents drag Hard Charger away.

"He's sharing a cell with an alien who farts every fifteen minutes," Alex said. "I'd tell the world you were Supergirl to get out of that situation." She gave her sister a teasing smile.

Kara smirked. "Nice to know your breaking point comes from a Casa de Grasa burrito."

J'onn approached them, still as Flamethrower. "It's time to go."

"Good luck!" called Alex, as J'onn, Kara, and Mon-El approached the balcony. "Don't get caught."

Kara hooked her arm through Mon-El's and took off, with J'onn quickly catching up.

"Let's land behind the theater," said J'onn, flying beside her.

Kara nodded. The DEO had been monitoring the Imperial Theater since they'd discovered the hideout. All the Dominants seemed to enter and exit through the loading dock.

J'onn hooked his arm through Kara's to give the illusion that she was carrying both Flamethrower and Hard Charger, and the trio touched down. J'onn approached the loading dock door first, hand on one hip in his sassiest pose, and Kara couldn't help but smile.

Just as they'd seen people do in the surveillance footage, J'onn knocked three times, then paused, and then knocked five times.

"Who's there?" a young female voice asked from the other side of the door.

"It's Elaine," said J'onn. "From apartment 404. I've got some other tenants with me who want to help."

Kara used her X-ray vision to see through the door. The little Braidzilla who'd attacked Supergirl with her hair had the remainder of it tucked under a ball cap and was talking to the Human Sponge.

Kara held her breath until the man nodded, and Braidzilla shifted the latch to unlock the dock door.

As the door rolled up, the Human Sponge studied all three members of the DEO team.

"So where have you two been?" he asked J'onn and Mon-El. "Elaine, your husband's been worrying like crazy. Why didn't you tell him you were coming?"

"We've been in hiding," answered J'onn. "I couldn't risk contacting him."

The Human Sponge nodded and pointed at Kara. "And who's this? I don't recognize you from Shady Oaks."

"I'm Bianca," said Kara. "I'm, uh, his girlfriend." She linked arms with the stocky, hairy version of Mon-El.

The Human Sponge wrinkled his nose. "Really? You're with Bert?"

"Well, she ain't with Ernie," said Mon-El with a chuckle.

The Human Sponge stared at him.

Mon-El cleared his throat. "You know, like Bert and Ernie from *Sesame Street*? The show about sharing and trash can monsters?"

The Human Sponge snickered. "Yeah, that sounds about your intelligence level, Bert. Well, good for you, getting the girl." He nodded to Kara. "Do you have powers?"

In answer, she floated above the ground. "I can do this."

The Human Sponge rubbed his chin. "That might come in handy if we need to make a quick getaway."

"Getaway?" J'onn repeated, feigning concern. "Aren't we safe here?"

"We're fine for now, but at some point the cops are gonna catch wise." The Human Sponge glanced past the DEO team. "Which means you should probably come inside before anyone gets suspicious. This theater's supposed to be closed for renovations until next month."

Kara exchanged a glance with Mon-El. That explained how nobody else had discovered them yet.

"How have you been feeling?" the Human Sponge asked J'onn.

"Feeling?" J'onn repeated.

"You know, superpower side effects," said the Human Sponge. "Nosebleeds, fainting spells . . ."

"Yes, of course," said J'onn. "I did have a nosebleed, now that you mention it."

"Well, we've got a nurse in the control booth upstairs if you need first aid," said the Human Sponge. He pointed above them to the theater's catwalk.

"How many people are staying here?" asked Kara, glancing around at the stage lights and rigging. Most of the bulbs had been smashed, and the rigging was covered in slime.

"About twenty," said the Human Sponge. "We're still trying to track down the other tenants."

Alex's voice tickled Kara's ear. "See if you can find out what kind of powers they have."

"Am I the only person here who can fly?" Kara asked, following the Human Sponge across the loading dock.

"No, we've got a woman with a propeller on her back and a guy who can make himself weightless," said the Human Sponge. "Watch your step. Jake was on lookout a while ago, and his slime dripped all over the place."

"Lookout? Is he the one guarding the orichalcum?" asked Kara.

"Careful, Kara," Alex spoke in her ear.

"Yeah, ease your way in," said Winn.

The Human Sponge stopped and turned. "You know, you ask a lot of questions."

Kara picked up a hundred-pound rigging sandbag with one hand. "I just want to make sure I'm not wasting my time." She tossed the bag effortlessly—as though it contained marshmallows—to the Human Sponge, who almost collapsed under the weight. "Are you guarding the orichalcum carefully or not?"

The Human Sponge lowered the bag to the ground and raised his eyebrow in suspicion. "You have *two* powers?"

Oops.

Inwardly, Kara chided herself. Why did she have to show off?

"Tell him yes; you're a myrmecologist," Alex spoke into Kara's ear.

She adjusted her glasses and looked the Human Sponge in the eye. "Of course I do. I'm a mermaid-ologist."

Alex and Winn groaned in stereo.

"Myrmecologist!" they said in unison.

"You're a what?" the Human Sponge asked.

"A myrmecologist," Kara corrected.

"She studies ants," J'onn explained. "Queen ants, to be specific."

Winn hooted. "Look at the big brains on J'onn!"

The Human Sponge relaxed. "Oh, right. Because they can fly, and ants are really strong."

"Yep!" Kara nodded emphatically. "That's exactly why." She crossed her arms. "So is the orichalcum safe or not?"

"It's safe," said the Human Sponge. "We keep it with us in the orchestra pit."

They followed him backstage and down a set of stairs leading to a door. As soon as he opened it, the stench of body odor assaulted Kara's nostrils. She covered her mouth and nose, while beside her Mon-El coughed.

Fifteen heads swiveled in their direction and then just as quickly returned to their activities. Most of the people looked normal, but what they were doing to pass the time clearly wasn't.

A man with a deck of cards was building a house, but instead of a flimsy structure, he appeared to be fusing the makeshift walls together with a touch of his fingertips. A few people were playing a game rolling dice with levitation, with thunderous claps, or by making the floor shake. There was a woman doing one-fingered push-ups while a man sat on her back, eating a box of nails.

Kara did her best to take it all in for Winn and Alex.

"So much awesome in one room," whispered Winn.

"So much odor in one room," Kara said.

The Human Sponge smirked at her, unaware that the comment was directed at Winn. "Yeah, but it's the only place they can't see us while they're doing renovations. We're lucky this pit has a lid on it." He pointed to the pit filler over their heads.

"Is that why you smashed all the lightbulbs on the catwalk?" asked Kara.

"Nah. That was for our new guy, Shadow," said the Human Sponge. "He can't stand the light."

"Was he up there just now?" asked J'onn, pointing toward the catwalk.

"Yeah," the Human Sponge said with a chuckle. "He's kind of invisible, so be careful what you say about him."

"Elaine!" A man pushed through the others to reach J'onn.

It was Mr. Slick, the slimy guy in swim trunks who'd stolen the orichalcum.

Kara stepped between Mr. Slick and J'onn, whose eyes were wide with alarm.

"You must be Jake, Elaine's husband," Kara said, extending a hand to Mr. Slick.

She instantly regretted it when he covered her palm with goop as he shook it.

"Hey, nice to meet you. Excuse me." He slipped past Kara and grabbed J'onn around the middle.

"Elaine, my honey bear!" He went in for a kiss and J'onn winced at the slimy lips on his.

"Hello, husband," said J'onn.

Alex sighed. "Seriously, J'onn? That's the most romantic sentiment you can muster?"

Mr. Slick pulled away from J'onn with a perplexed look. "Hello, husband?"

J'onn closed his eyes, reaching into Mr. Slick's mind, and when he opened them again, said, "I mean . . . Snickerdoodlepoo."

Kara snorted a laugh, but Mr. Slick didn't notice. He was beaming at J'onn.

"That's better. Where have you been, honey bear?"

"I was hiding with friends." J'onn indicated Kara and

Mon-El. "I wasn't sure if it was really you just now. That's why I called you husband."

"Oh, right. Because Pete can change his appearance." Jake gestured to the far corner. "Well, come have a seat. You guys are welcome, too." He smiled at Kara and Mon-El.

"We'd love to," said Kara. "But I think my boyfriend and I would like to see the nurse first." She turned to the Human Sponge. "Where did you say she is?"

"Control booth," said the Human Sponge. "Take the ladder up to the catwalk, and it's across the theater."

"We'll be back soon," Kara told J'onn.

"Hurry," he said, forcing a smile. "You don't want to miss all the fun."

Kara and Mon-El left the orchestra pit and were back in the loading dock before Alex's voice spoke in Kara's ear again.

"We don't know where that Shadow guy could be hiding, so don't answer me out loud," said Alex. "But you need to find out how much the nurse knows about orichalcum. The people in the orchestra pit weren't afraid to use their powers, so either they don't know they'll be running out soon, or they've already figured it out and have been tapping into the orichalcum they stole from the museum."

Kara gave a slight nod of her head, and she and Mon-El climbed the ladder to the catwalk.

They quietly traversed the theater, and when Kara opened the control booth door, there were only two people in the room: a woman in hospital scrubs and a man lying on the floor.

"Hello," the woman greeted them with a pleasant smile. She held an IV bag of red-tinged fluid in one hand that was being dripped into the arm of the man on the floor. But the fluid wasn't blood.

Kara clutched at Mon-El's hand.

There was no question about it. The Dominants were definitely using the orichalcum.

"I can't believe they're using more orichalcum." Alex's forehead wrinkled with worry. "How are they not getting even sicker?"

Kara and Mon-El were back at the DEO, discussing their recon mission with Alex, Winn, and James, who'd returned from CatCo.

"Apparently, when the nurse gives them an orichalcum refill, she also throws in something called dactinomycin," said Kara.

"Dactino . . ." Alex sighed and buried her face in her hands. "Doctors use that to treat chemotherapy patients. It *kills* white blood cells."

"Well, no white blood cells would mean nothing attacks the orichalcum," pointed out James.

"Yes, but it also means the people taking it can get life-threatening infections much easier," said Alex.

"I tried to tell the nurse orichalcum was bad," said Kara, shrugging. "She seems to think people are getting sick from *not* having enough."

"When it's really the opposite," said James. He folded his hands in front of him. "All right. Give me the antidote."

His request earned looks of surprise. So far, nobody had told him the antidote merely stopped the onslaught of white blood cells—that it didn't affect a person's power at all.

Which meant James was truly willing to give up his power.

"You want to take the antidote?" asked Kara.

James smiled at her shocked expression. "I've been thinking about it a lot today. This orichalcum affects people, physically and mentally." He shook his head. "A superpower would be nice, but not if it costs me who I already am."

"Aw, James!" Kara leaned over and hugged him. "That's so great to hear." She adjusted her glasses. "But this antidote won't take your power. It just keeps the orichalcum from causing a dangerous overreaction in the body."

Instead of the whoop of joy she expected, James nodded solemnly. "Then we'd better take advantage of my power while I still have it."

"I couldn't agree more." J'onn's voice carried down the steps as he entered the control room in his Hank Henshaw form. "Time is now working against us."

Alex got to her feet. "J'onn! What are you doing here?"

"I convinced Mr. Slick and the others that I was going to recruit more supercitizens to join them. *After* they informed me of their plans to replicate the orichalcum."

"Replicate it?" Kara frowned. "That's not possible."

J'onn sat on the edge of Winn's desk. "How are people getting their superpowers, Miss Danvers?"

Kara hesitated before answering. "It comes from whatever they're focused on." Then she groaned and bowed her head. "So why not focus on replicating the orichalcum?"

"Exactly."

"Yeah, but to create something with that much power . . ." Alex shook her head. "That could be lethal."

"It *has* been lethal," J'onn said, clenching his jaw. "Since the Dominants already have powers, they tried recruiting an outsider to do it—a sister of one of the tenants. The blood in her body boiled, and she died."

Kara and Alex clapped hands over their mouths, and James and Mon-El stared at the floor.

"But they're going to try again, aren't they?" Winn asked in a tremulous voice.

"Until they get it right," said J'onn. "Or until someone stops them."

Alex narrowed her eyes. "Then that's what we'll do."

"What are you thinking, Agent Danvers?" asked J'onn.

"We let them go to sleep. Lull them into a false sense of security, and just before dawn, we strike," Alex said.

"Even with all our field agents, that's fifteen of our people—only some of whom have powers—to their twenty, *all* of whom have powers," said J'onn. "They have us outnumbered and outmatched."

Winn raised his hand. "Not if we take up the offers of the supercitizens who called the hotline to help."

"Yeah, right," Alex scoffed. "We can't ask innocent people to risk their lives." She looked to Kara for agreement, but Kara was tapping her fingertips against her lower lip.

"I think it's a good idea," she finally said.

"What?!" Alex exclaimed.

Winn pumped his fist. "Yes! Superbattle!"

Kara zipped around the corner and returned as Supergirl. "I'll start recruiting!"

"No way," said Alex, waving her arms. "We cannot get them involved."

"Why not? It sounds good to me," said Mon-El.

"Me, too," said James.

J'onn remained oddly quiet.

"This city isn't just ours to protect, Alex," said Supergirl. The realization was starting to hit her. All those citizens she'd scolded for using their powers . . . they just wanted to make a difference.

"National City belongs to everyone out there, too." Supergirl pointed to the skyline. "Yes, things might get dangerous, but if these supercitizens fight beside us, I think we can win. They know the people they're up against. They might even be able to get them to stand down."

"I don't know . . ." Alex's arms relaxed at her side, but her expression was pained.

Supergirl touched a hand to the *S* on her chest. "Stronger together, Alex. All of us."

Alex sighed and gestured to J'onn. "It's up to the big boss."

Everyone turned to J'onn, who had his hands clasped behind his back.

"Mr. Schott," he said, "do you still have the phone numbers for those supercitizens who want to help?"

Winn flashed a stack of papers. "Absolutely."

J'onn nodded. "Then let's find out what they're capable of."

# 15

**T**HERE ARE SERIOUSLY A LOT OF abandoned warehouses in this city," Mon-El said, gazing at the cavernous space around him.

He, Supergirl, James, and Winn had been told to meet there while J'onn and Alex gathered the volunteer supercitizens the team had chosen.

"Yeah, whenever we find a baddie hiding in one of these, we mark the location in case it gets used again," Winn said, picking at a rust chip on the wall. "I never thought we'd be using it ourselves, though."

The warehouse doors creaked open, and in walked J'onn and Alex, followed by six people in DEO uniforms.

The supercitizens stopped when they saw Supergirl, their

expressions turning to either awe or annoyance. Apparently, even though Supergirl and her friends knew who *they'd* be working with, the same wasn't true of the supercitizens.

"You didn't say Supergirl would be here." Jacqueline Reyes, the meteorologist, scowled, hands on hips. "I seem to recall her telling us to stay out of the way."

"Yeah, she picked me up and flew me to a different part of town," said Reshma, the cat controller. "I couldn't even *try* to fix the mess I made."

Eddy, a solar flare researcher who'd become the physical embodiment of sunlight, took a tentative step forward. "I can't believe I'm in the same room as Supergirl!" There was a crackling sound, and Eddy started to glow.

"Let's save it for later." J'onn put a hand on Eddy's shoulder and instantly jerked it back. "Blazes, that's hot!"

"Yeah, that happens." Eddy kicked at the floor. "I accidentally burned my bed up this morning."

"How have you not burned through your uniform?" asked James.

"Flame-retardant polymers," said Winn, winking. "Designed by yours truly."

"Anyway, it's an honor to meet you." Eddy waved to Supergirl; she smiled and waved back.

"Thank you for helping us," she said. "All of you." Her

gaze took in each supercitizen. "You're right to be upset with me. I haven't been very reasonable toward supercitizens." She paced in front of them. "You want to protect your city. I get that. I respect that. And, as a friend reminded me—" she glanced at James and smiled—"I wasn't so great at saving the day when I first started.

"I'd like us to save this city together," Supergirl continued, "if you'll have me on your team."

"Absolutely!" said Eddy.

"Why not?" Marcus from Noonan's said with a shrug.

There was a moment of silence as the remaining supercitizens looked at one another, and then Jacqueline stepped forward, hand extended.

"It would be a privilege to work with you," she told Supergirl.

The remaining supercitizens murmured their approval.

Supergirl smiled and shook Jacqueline's hand. "Thank you. I'll see if we can get a weather observatory named after you."

Jacqueline returned her smile. "Not a weather observatory. But a park bench maybe." She stepped aside, and Eddy took her place.

"I'm . . . it's just . . ." Eddy's face started to glow again, and he tucked his hands behind his back.

"Don't worry, I can take the heat." Supergirl extended her hand with a giggle. Eddy shook it and hurried away, grinning.

"I *have* been practicing with cats, just like you suggested," said Reshma as she approached Supergirl.

Supergirl winced and squeezed Reshma's hand. "I shouldn't have flown you out of there like I did. I'm sorry."

Reshma put a hand over Supergirl's. "You were right. I wasn't ready."

Supergirl glanced past Reshma. "So, did you bring a feline friend?"

"A few," said Reshma with a smile. "They'll come when I call."

"Well, we're happy to have you. And them," Supergirl told Reshma.

After each supercitizen greeted Supergirl, Alex called them over to give them the orichalcum antidote while Mon-El checked their orichalcum levels using special goggles Winn and Dr. Wanabi had created: the Atlantis Eyes.

"Do they know this battle might use the last of their powers?" Mon-El asked Alex in a low voice. He'd just scanned Jacqueline, whose silhouette couldn't have contained more than 25 percent orichalcum.

She nodded. "It's a sacrifice they're willing to make."

With newfound respect, Mon-El watched everyone

who approached Supergirl. He could live without the shape-shifting ability he'd gained from the orichalcum, but the powers he'd gained from the Earth's yellow sun . . . he couldn't imagine life without those. It was why he'd been willing to talk to Kara on James's behalf.

"You OK?" Alex asked him.

He nodded. "Just thinking that I couldn't have picked a better city to crash-land in."

Alex smiled until she turned and saw Eddy approaching, face still aglow. She held her hands up. "Whoa. Let's calm down a bit or you'll melt this needle before it even gets into your skin." She wiggled the antidote syringe.

"Sorry, but I'm fighting crime with Supergirl!" Eddy gave a fist pump. "She's amazing."

Mon-El grinned. "She really is, isn't she? Have you seen her use her freeze breath?"

Eddy clasped his hands together. "That is the best!"

Alex squinted as Eddy's face brightened even further. "Mon-El? Not helping."

"Sorry! Think of sad things," he told Eddy. "Like melted ice cream or a three-legged kitten or . . ." Mon-El's gaze wandered to Marcus, who was grinning rakishly at Supergirl. "A guy hitting on your girlfriend *and* her alter ego."

Eddy frowned. "Huh?" But in his confusion, his skin

returned to normal, so Alex seized the opportunity to administer his shot.

"Mon-El? Can you check Eddy's power reserves?" she asked, grabbing Mon-El's arm and turning him away from Supergirl.

Mon-El slipped the goggles on and examined Eddy's silhouette. "You haven't used your power much, have you?" He raised the goggles and told Alex, "He's almost as red as Supergirl was when we checked her."

"Is that a good thing?" asked Eddy at the raised eyebrows from Alex.

"Just stay close to me and Supergirl with that sunlight, new best friend." Mon-El put an arm around Eddy.

Supergirl glanced over and snickered.

"Your laugh is really familiar," Marcus told her. "Do you ever go to Noonan's restaurant?"

Supergirl stopped laughing. "Do I . . . Noonan's?" She shook her head vehemently. "Never. I hate coffee. And food!" she added, realizing he hadn't specifically mentioned coffee. She pumped his hand and steered him toward Alex. "Anyway, thanks for your help. Agent Danvers will shoot you now. Uh, I mean, give you a shot now," she corrected with a cringe.

She turned to the next supercitizen, a shy teenage boy who was hugging himself.

"Hey! You must be Matt. Your power seems pretty cool!" Supergirl reached out to lightly punch his shoulder, but her fist passed right through him.

"Sorry," he said. "Reflex." He jammed his eyes shut and then opened them, offering a now-solid hand to Supergirl, who shook it. "I really want to help."

"Good! Because we've got big plans for you," said Supergirl.

"For all of us?" The last of the supercitizens, a college-age girl, walked over.

"You're Becca, right?" Supergirl shook her hand. According to her bio, she was a film student who could animate any object she touched.

Becca nodded. "So what are we going to do?"

The other supercitizens and the DEO team were now all watching and waiting for Supergirl's response.

"You want to know what we're going to do?" Supergirl crossed her arms and raised her chin. "We're going to show the Dominants who's strong, who's powerful, and who protects this city!"

"Yeah!" everyone else hooted and applauded.

After the commotion died down, Marcus raised a hand. "It's us, right?"

# 16

**W**HILE MOST OF NATIONAL CITY slept, a line of black-and-white police cars formed a one-block perimeter around the Imperial Theater.

"I could only convince the police chief to give you this much manpower for half an hour." Maggie showed Alex and Supergirl the car placement on her tablet. The DEO team and supercitizens were at a diner across from the theater, discussing final plans. "After thirty minutes, they roll out."

Alex squeezed Maggie's arm. "Thank you so much. For everything." She reached into her utility bag and pulled out a beribboned box of tiramisu. "Your reward, as promised."

Maggie laughed and put a hand over Alex's. "Just make sure you get out of there in one piece."

At the counter, a man in a velour track suit waved his hands dramatically as he talked to J'onn, who listened with a stoic expression.

"You never said anything about holding your firefight in my theater!" The man in the track suit jabbed himself in the chest. "I've poured my heart and soul into that place!"

"It won't be a firefight, Mr. Albright," J'onn assured him. "My team and I will be using stun guns. No bullets. We want to get those people out of your building as safely and quietly as you do."

Mr. Albright stroked the stubble on his chin several times. "No bullets, no collateral damage. That's good."

J'onn snorted. "Oh, I never said that. We'll do our best to keep the damage to a minimum, but things will break."

Mr. Albright's hand dropped to his side. "What?!"

Supergirl cleared her throat and joined them. "Mr. Albright, hi!" She gave him her best smile. "I'm Supergirl."

"Yes, of course I know who you are, dear." He patted her shoulder. "And I'm in awe of your presence." He looked at J'onn. "But I'm also in awe of what you're telling me!"

*You're saving lives, but at my expense!* was the echo Supergirl caught.

"You want to know what's in it for you?" she asked, recalling her conversation with Mon-El.

Mr. Albright nodded.

"Your theater is about to be the famed site of a battle between supercitizens," Supergirl said matter-of-factly.

Mr. Albright uncrossed his arms. "Famed?"

Supergirl nodded. "How much do you think people will pay to see where it all happened and maybe own a piece of it?" She leaned in. "Anything we damage becomes an instant souvenir."

Supergirl could practically hear the *ka-ching!* of a cash register in Mr. Albright's brain.

Alex joined them. "And that's not counting the extra money you'll get from your insurance for damages. You could do a bigger and better remodeling of that theater than you originally planned."

Mr. Albright stared into the distance, grinning as he pulled out a set of keys from his pocket. "The one with the blue cap is for the side door to the theater."

J'onn took the keys from him. "Thank you. We'll contact you when we're finished." He pocketed the keys and glanced around at the supercitizens and DEO team. "Alex, ready the troops."

"OK!" Alex clapped her hands. "Let's go over the mission parameters once more. The DEO strike team, Supergirl, Mon-El, and Guardian will move in first with J'onn and me. Supercitizens, Winn will tell you when to follow."

She gestured to Winn, who saluted the supercitizens

from a booth crowded with his laptop, a communications system, a police scanner, and two massive monitors.

"Once the conflict begins, there will be a DEO van parked behind the theater," Alex continued. "If you apprehend any Dominants, take them to the van, where Dr. Wanabi will be waiting to treat them—and an NCPD officer will be waiting to take them into custody." She gestured to Dr. Wanabi and Maggie, respectively. "If you don't know how much power you have left, Guardian will be wearing the Atlantis Eyes. You can check with him."

Guardian tapped the goggles and gave everyone a thumbs-up.

"It's important to remember that these are mortal human beings," said J'onn. "Our mission is to disarm and arrest. Use extreme force *only* in extreme circumstances. Good luck." Without another word, he pushed open the diner door and walked outside.

Alex, Supergirl, Mon-El, and Guardian followed, along with the DEO team. Once they'd crossed the street, J'onn looked to Supergirl. She narrowed her eyes and peered through the concrete back wall of the theater. Three people guarded the loading dock door, but none of them acted as if anything was out of the ordinary.

"Three guards, this end," she told him, pointing to the loading dock.

He nodded and transformed into Martian Manhunter, bedecked in black body armor with a red *X* across the chest. "Operation Ruby begins now," he said, disappearing around the corner of the building.

Supergirl used her X-ray vision to follow him. Once she saw him flash a thumbs-up, she turned her attention to the Dominants guarding the loading dock. Her superhearing picked up a smattering of conversation, which was quickly drowned out by a clattering and grunting.

"What was that?" one of the Dominants asked.

"Uh-oh," said Supergirl.

Alex raised her eyebrows. "What oh?"

Supergirl put a finger to her lips and scanned the interior for J'onn. He seemed to be wrestling with someone, but Supergirl couldn't actually see anybody. She could, however, see the three people guarding the door leave to join the fight.

"Looks like our covert op isn't so covert anymore," said Supergirl. "J'onn needs our help."

"Remember," Winn spoke over comms, "don't just fight them; drain their powers."

Alex smirked at her sister. "You heard the man. Let's shut 'em down."

Supergirl raised a leg and kicked out hard, sending the door flying across the loading dock. She, Alex, Mon-El, and Guardian burst inside, with the DEO agents behind them.

Supergirl spotted a Dominant dressed all in black lying unconscious on the floor. Three more Dominants were gathered around J'onn, who was punching and kicking with all his might.

They all turned at the sudden entrance, but only two of the Dominants ran over. The third one, skin covered in prickly barbs, continued to rain punches on J'onn, his spiky fists leaving puncture marks in J'onn's skin with every blow.

The other two Dominants made their powers immediately apparent. One of them waved at the floor beneath Mon-El and Guardian. A portal appeared, and Supergirl's boyfriend and best friend *dis*appeared.

"Mon-El! James!" Supergirl shouted.

"We're outside," Mon-El's voice came through her earpiece a few seconds later. "But we're on our way back!"

"That portal maker is quick with the egress," Winn commented through their earpieces. "Hey! I think we just found his nickname."

A female Dominant charged at two DEO agents, who fired their stun guns. But instead of bringing her down, the electrical discharges only seemed to annoy her. She roared and lowered her shoulder, barreling into the agents and sending them flying. With a satisfied grunt, she wheeled around and charged toward Alex and the other agents.

"So this is what a bullfight's like," muttered Alex.

Egress, the portal maker, waved his hand at the floor under Supergirl, and she leaped into the air.

"Sorry, but you've got the wrong girl," she said smugly.

"I might, but he doesn't." Egress smiled and pointed above them.

Two more Dominants were running along the catwalk. One of them flexed his fingers at Supergirl and darts whistled through the air, aimed at her extremities.

So this was Digits.

Supergirl curled up in midair and covered herself with her cape. The darts bounced off harmlessly, but *someone* leaped from the catwalk and onto Supergirl's back. Unprepared for a passenger, she plummeted to the ground, and the passenger rolled off.

"Thanks for the ride," said a woman's voice, accompanied by a clattering of wood.

Flinging back her cape, Supergirl watched the woman shrink and mutate until she resembled a marionette.

"Stringleshanks," hissed Supergirl.

The puppet sprinted for Alex and the DEO agents with a knife in each hand.

"Incoming, Alex!" said Supergirl.

"Leave her to me," said Guardian as he and Mon-El ran into the theater.

But before Guardian could even get close, Egress gestured at the floor again. Mon-El was quick enough to jump aside, but Guardian disappeared once more.

Alex groaned. "James, you've got to stop falling into his trap!"

"Actually," said Guardian, "I think I need to keep doing exactly what I'm doing." Supergirl could hear him breathing hard as he ran back toward the theater.

Meanwhile, Mon-El was toying with Digits, dashing from side to side using his superspeed, so that each dart missed him by several feet.

"Wow, you have terrible aim," Mon-El told him. "Have you considered glasses?"

Digits sneered and unleashed another volley of projectiles at Mon-El, who expertly avoided them all.

"I think I'd go for square frames if I were you," said Mon-El, pointing to his eyes. "Maybe heart-shaped."

Supergirl snickered and flew after Stringleshanks. Using her heat vision, Supergirl zapped the puppet on each hand, forcing her to drop the knives.

Stringleshanks twisted her head around to smirk at Supergirl. "You really think that's all I've got?"

The marionette reached over one shoulder and uncoiled a long wire, snapping it taut and leaping at Supergirl. Supergirl's right hand whipped up and caught

Stringleshanks by the neck, but the puppet merely tightened her wire around Supergirl's wrist, cutting off the circulation.

"You can't choke me out," chuckled Stringleshanks. "I've got no bones for you to break! Unless you burn me alive, you can't defeat me."

Supergirl tried to clobber the marionette with her free hand, but Stringleshanks went limp and slipped to the floor.

"I hate puppets," Supergirl grumbled as Stringleshanks scurried to pick up her knives.

J'onn, who'd finally bested the barb-covered man, ran over to help Alex deal with the bullish woman while the remaining DEO agents lay unconscious around her.

"Guardian, I need a power update!" J'onn barked.

"Your new opponent is at twenty-five percent, Stringleshanks is at fifty percent, Digits is at fifteen percent, and Egress is at forty percent," Guardian said. "But he's about to be at zero."

"Winn, send in the backup team," said J'onn.

"You got it, boss!"

Guardian ran up to Egress, who clucked his tongue and gestured at the floor. Guardian jumped and dropped his shield, which touched the portal, causing it to close.

"Smart," said Egress. "But I'm smarter." He gestured once more, and Guardian fell through another hole. Then

Egress moved the hole under *Mon-El*'s feet just as a fistful of darts were about to hit him.

"Hey, tell Egress thanks!" Mon-El's voice sounded in Supergirl's ear. "He just saved my life."

"Yeah, his partner's not so happy about that." Supergirl glanced at Digits, who was shouting at Egress.

Digits gestured angrily—and then frowned when nothing flew from his fingertips. He massaged his hand and tried again, but still nothing appeared.

"Looks like someone's fifteen minutes of fame are up." Supergirl flew to the catwalk and nabbed Digits, carrying him to the DEO van, where Dr. Wanabi and Maggie were waiting.

"Here's your first patient and prisoner," she told them, zooming back into the theater.

Guardian was once again making a beeline for Egress, who rolled his eyes.

"You know, the definition of stupidity is doing the same thing over and over, expecting different results," he told Guardian, pointing at the floor.

No portal appeared.

"That's the definition of insanity," Guardian said. "Stupidity is not realizing when you've been played for your powers." And with a swing of one elbow, he knocked Egress out.

"Nice job!" Supergirl cheered.

"You may have weakened *us*," said Stringleshanks, who was starting to look more human than wooden. "But there are only five of you now, and we've already sent someone for backup." She glanced to the corner, and so did Supergirl.

The unconscious Dominant in black was gone. Footsteps thundered along the catwalk and from the stage area of the theater.

"They'll be here any second," Stringleshanks said with a smug smile, brandishing a knife.

"Please." Supergirl snorted. "You really don't think *we* came prepared?" She gestured toward the loading dock entrance just as Mon-El charged back into the theater with the supercitizens behind him.

Becca, the animator, waved at the stage rigging, which came to life and wound itself around Stringleshanks, lifting her into the air. Becca smiled—but it quickly turned to a look of surprise as she was flung onto her stomach, braids wrapped around her ankles.

"Lucky for me, hair grows," said Braidzilla.

Alex ran to help Becca, but a woman outfitted with a propeller swooped down and tackled Alex. The Dominant and the DEO agent exchanged blows. Then, just as the flying woman lifted Alex off the ground, Reshma appeared.

Along with twenty cats.

"I hear she's got catnip on her," Reshma told her feline friends, pointing to the flying woman. "Take her down!"

The cats yowled and jumped on the flying woman, who dropped Alex and tried to flee, only to have her propellers ravaged by tiny teeth and claws.

A swarm of bees zipped through the rear stage curtains, but Supergirl blocked them with her cape. As they headed for Alex, Matt the intangible waved his arms and taunted Bee Breather.

"Can't catch me!" he shouted, running away.

The bees swarmed after him, and Matt kept running until he reached the loading dock wall. Pressing his back against it, he turned himself transparent at the last second. All the bees collided with one another or the concrete.

"Nice job, Matt!" Supergirl cheered, and then grunted as she was struck between the shoulder blades. She started to topple forward, but something held her waist in a viselike grip. Supergirl twisted around to see her latest opponent.

She wished she hadn't.

Nothing about this guy, except his shirt and pants, seemed human. His arms were wrenches, his legs were needle-nose pliers, and his head was a massive hammer.

"I'm about to fight a toolbox," she murmured in amazement.

The hammer swung down, connecting with the side of

Supergirl's head, and for a moment stars speckled her vision. With both arms still free, she threw a left-right punch combo, hoping to connect with some sort of flesh, but her knuckles throbbed as they met metal.

One of the wrench arms still held her, while the other reeled back. Supergirl raised her arms to block the hit just as Digits trotted over.

"Hey, metal head! What are you doing here?" He frowned at Toolbox.

"What are *you* doing here?" Supergirl asked Digits. "I put you in the DEO van!"

"Cram it, Supergross," he shot back. He turned to Toolbox. "The boss wants you outside, so drop this chick and get going. I'll finish her off." He sneered at Supergirl.

Toolbox released her and hobbled away, leaving Supergirl to rub her sides and smirk at the dart flinger.

"Supergross? That was the best you could come up with?" Digits grinned as he changed back into Mon-El.

"That gave me away, didn't it?" Mon-El asked.

"Just a little." Supergirl glanced past him. "And you realize you sent that walking toolbox outside where we have friends."

"Who will very soon have an electromagnet," Winn's voice sounded in Supergirl's ear. "Courtesy of a car battery, some speakers, and yours truly."

"You rock, Winn!" said Supergirl.

"Nah," he said with a chuckle. "Basic junior high—"

"Uh, guys? We're about to have a situation here," interrupted Mon-El.

A half-dozen more Dominants joined the fray, leaping, flying, sliding, or running to the scene.

"Shades on!" J'onn shouted to his team and the supercitizens. They quickly obeyed, slipping on Winn-enhanced sunglasses.

Reshma commanded her cats to scatter, and J'onn turned to Eddy. "Light it up, Mr. Lee."

Eddy grinned and shone so brightly, Supergirl could feel the heat on her cheeks. She also felt the sunlight invigorate every inch of her body. Beside her, Mon-El grinned and stretched his muscles.

The Dominants made sounds of protest and shielded their eyes, allowing the DEO team and supercitizens to sneak in a few more attacks. Marcus picked up the bullish woman and hurled her across the loading dock, through the curtains, and onto the stage.

Supergirl winced. "Maybe a lighter toss next time," she told him.

Marcus frowned. "That *was* a light toss."

Suddenly the room was plunged into darkness.

"Eddy?" Supergirl glanced around. She took off her sunglasses, letting her eyes adjust to the dim lighting.

"Sorry. I'm tapped out," he said sheepishly.

The rest of the DEO team and supercitizens took off their sunglasses, and the Dominants resumed their attack, though they were the worse for wear.

Before Supergirl could get her hands on a guy who appeared to be eating all their weapons, she felt a tap on her shoulder.

"Supergirl," Reshma whispered in her ear, "the cats say only one person is guarding the orichalcum in the orchestra pit."

Supergirl raised her eyebrows and used her X-ray vision to take in the Dominants in the area. No sign of the one dressed in black.

"Would you mind taking care of the guy with the bottomless stomach?" she asked Reshma. "I've got a promise to keep."

"Not at all," said Reshma.

Supergirl shot through the backstage curtain and thrust her fist in front of her, punching her way through the orchestra pit filler. When she touched down and saw who was guarding the orichalcum, she groaned.

"Not you again!"

The Human Sponge grinned at her. "Hit me with your best shot."

Supergirl scowled. "Gladly." She drew back her fist and

punched, but as expected, the Human Sponge just stood there.

He crossed his arms. "I said your *best* shot, girly," he taunted.

"Winn," Supergirl said under her breath, "how do I beat the Human Sponge?"

"The Human Sponge?" repeated the Human Sponge, making a face. "That's what people are calling me?"

"Remember, he's only invulnerable as long as he has his powers," said Winn. "Bring them down, and he's just a regular guy."

"So I have to punch the power out of him?" Supergirl asked with a sigh. "That could take the rest of the night."

"Why not call me the Shock Absorber?" asked the Human Sponge. "Or the Wall?"

Supergirl punched him three times in rapid succession just to quiet him for a moment.

"His power can absorb a lot of damage," said Winn.

"I know that, Winn!" Supergirl said in exasperation. "That's the problem!"

"No, Kara. That's the solution. His power can absorb a *lot*. If you hit him with something that would kill most people, he'll use all his power protecting himself and he won't even know it."

Supergirl's eyes widened. "Ohhh."

The Human Sponge was pacing in front of the orichalcum. "I mean, I've heard people calling my neighbor Lady Levitation, so why—"

Supergirl took a deep breath, and released an icy blast, freezing the Human Sponge in place. She waited and watched his power absorb cold that would kill a normal human being. When she saw his fingers start to turn blue, she blasted him with her heat vision.

"—the Human Sponge?" he finished as he thawed out, oblivious to what had happened. "I mean, you've gotta give me something here." He held his arms open, and Supergirl smiled at him.

"OK," she said.

She reeled back her fist, and the Human Sponge smirked.

Supergirl's punch connected, and he wobbled on the spot, pointing at her.

"Hey, how did you—" The Human Sponge fell backward against the table that held the orichalcum.

But when the table fell, there was no clinking of metal on metal.

The orichalcum was gone.

Supergirl smiled.

"Winn, someone took the orichalcum," she said. "Can you track it?"

"Absolutely," he said, and Supergirl heard the clacking

of keys. "The orichalcum has left the building. It's in a white SUV beyond the police perimeter heading down Seventh Street."

Supergirl flew out of the orchestra pit and through the front doors of the theater, zooming along Seventh Street.

She spotted the white SUV and flew up to the driver's window, knocking on the glass.

A man dressed all in black gave her a startled look.

"Hi, Shadow!" she called. "Why don't you take a left at the next light and head for the police station?"

Shadow stepped on the gas and turned right instead. Supergirl gave chase for a few blocks and then approached the passenger side of the SUV. Shadow veered hard left.

"He's falling for it!" Winn said in a gleeful voice.

Supergirl herded Shadow's SUV a couple more blocks, always giving him a slight lead, all the way to the harbor.

Once he reached the waterfront, Shadow jumped out of his SUV and put on the pack filled with orichalcum. Just as Supergirl was closing in, Shadow ran for a speedboat tied to the dock and started it up. With a grin and a salute at Supergirl, he revved the motor and headed out into the ocean.

Supergirl floated in the air, arms crossed, watching him race away.

The speedboat met fairly calm water until about fifty yards out. Then a geyser exploded next to Shadow's boat, and from the center of it emerged . . . Pryll. Shadow gave a terrified shriek as Pryll leaped over the boat, grabbing both supercitizen and orichalcum and pulling them underwater.

The ocean continued to bubble and froth for several minutes until it went calm once more, gentle waves slapping against the remains of an empty backpack that floated to the surface.

The guardian of Atlantis had fulfilled his duty.

# 17

"ELL, THE THEATER'S STILL standing and nobody's dead," said Winn. "I'd call that a . . ." He pointed to himself.

"I don't think Mr. Albright would agree," said James with a smirk. "I saw him crying in the theater parking lot when we drove away."

The sun had finally risen, and they were back at DEO headquarters, along with Alex and Mon-El, who were awaiting their debriefings by J'onn.

"Maybe they were tears of joy," suggested Mon-El.

Alex snorted. "Yeah, because he was happy to see us leave."

"At least he has plenty of souvenirs to sell." Supergirl walked over from the debriefing room. "Babe, you're up."

She rattled the back of Mon-El's chair.

He sighed and stood. "I still don't know why I have to do this. J'onn was there. He knows what happened."

"Oh, really?" Alex cocked her head to one side. "He was there when you ran onto the stage and swung over the orchestra pit on a curtain before crashing into the front row of seats?"

Mon-El pressed his lips together. "That's actually her fault." He pointed a thumb at Supergirl, who made a sputtering sound.

"Me? How?" she asked.

"You took me to see that pirate movie," said Mon-El. "You know I'm easily influenced by the reckless actions of others."

Supergirl glanced at Alex, who shrugged. "You can't argue with logic like that."

"Plus, I wasn't thinking straight." Mon-El grabbed Supergirl's hand. "I was worried about you chasing the supercitizen alone."

She beamed at him. "Well, as you can see, everything turned out fine."

Alex crossed her arms. "I still think you should've told all of us your plan with Pryll, not just Winn. We could've helped."

Supergirl shook her head. "The more people knew, the

more complicated it would've gotten. Besides, I also told J'onn. I needed him to put Shadow in a chokehold that would only knock him out for a few minutes."

Alex's mouth fell open. "When did you do that?"

"When you were giving your speech at the diner," Supergirl said with a grin.

"But what if Shadow had escaped with the orichalcum while everyone was fighting?" asked James.

Supergirl nodded to Winn. "That's why I told Winn the plan—so he could keep an eye on the orichalcum. If it moved too early, he'd let me know."

J'onn appeared in the doorway of the debriefing room. "Mon-El?"

"Sorry, coming!" Mon-El blew Supergirl a kiss and jogged away.

"I do wish you guys could've seen Pryll's moment of glory." Supergirl took Mon-El's vacant chair. "He leaped out of the water, grabbed Shadow and the orichalcum, and dove right back under." She mimed the jump with her hand. "If it'd been an Olympic event, I would've given him a 9.8."

Alex and Winn laughed, but James didn't. "Wait a minute. He took someone underwater with him?" James turned to Winn. "I thought you said nobody died."

"Nobody did," confirmed Winn, turning toward his

computer. He punched a couple of keys, and an image of a bedraggled, waterlogged Shadow appeared on-screen. "About fifteen minutes ago, the Coast Guard found this man floating on driftwood, raving about an underwater city."

The concerned look on James's face didn't ease. "What if they start looking for Atlantis?"

Winn gestured to Supergirl, who got back to her feet.

"That's where I come in," she said.

Winn opened his desk drawer and, with a Herculean effort, hefted out what looked like three shot-putting spheres.

"These are signal blockers that will prevent sonar, radar, lidar, and every-other-kind-of-ar from ever finding Atlantis again," said Winn.

Supergirl picked up the blockers as easily as if they were golf balls. "I'll let you know once I hand them over to Pryll."

"Do you want to get coffee when you're done there?" asked Alex, yawning. "I'm gonna need a pick-me-up."

"I'd love to, but I've still got a mayor's office to visit and one more article to write." She stifled a yawn of her own and took off for National City Harbor.

Supergirl retraced the speedboat's earlier path, pausing in her flight once she'd reached the point where Pryll had appeared. Making sure there were no ships around, she dipped low and rapid-punched the water three times, hard enough to create a slew of waves.

Then she waited.

After a couple of minutes, her eyes caught movement in the water, and then Pryll's head broke the surface.

"Supergirl, it is nice to see you," he said by way of greeting.

"Hi, Pryll," she said with a smile. "I brought something to protect your city." She held up the signal blockers. "Plant them on three corners of Atlantis, and nobody should bother you again."

Pryll reached up and took them from her. "Thank you, Supergirl. For this *and* for keeping your promise."

"Thank you for trusting me. And for not killing that guy you captured," she said with a smirk.

Pryll nodded solemnly. "You are a friend of Atlantis. We keep our promises, too."

"Well, I'm . . ." Supergirl stopped. "Wait a minute. Did you say 'we'?"

Pryll floated quietly for a moment.

"Pryll?" Supergirl coaxed.

"I was not entirely forthright with you earlier," he said. "You assumed I was the last of my kind. That is untrue. My king also lives."

Supergirl's eyes widened. "There's a king of Atlantis?"

"He is reluctant to rule, but yes."

Supergirl crossed her arms and smiled at Pryll. "You tricked me."

He smiled back. "I gained more of your sympathy when you thought I was alone. Would you still have helped otherwise?"

"Of course," she said. "But I *am* glad you're not the last of your kind." She pressed a hand to her chest. "Be well, Pryll of Atlantis."

He imitated her gesture. "Be well, Supergirl."

Pryll submerged, and Supergirl watched his dark form until it disappeared into the darker depths of the ocean.

As she shot into the sky, Supergirl smiled to herself.

If she could finally make peace with a nearly extinct sea species, apologizing to the mayor's assistant would be a piece of cake.

And speaking of cake . . .

Supergirl zipped across the country to a bakery and coffee shop in Central City, wondering if her friend Barry Allen had a CC Jitters on *his* Earth. She snatched up some pastries, dropped money on the counter, and flew back to her own city. After ducking into an alley behind City Hall, she reemerged as Kara Danvers, carrying three pink bakery boxes.

When she entered the building, Kara handed one of the boxes to the guards, thanking them for their service. The next box she brought to Ms. Binder's desk. Thankfully, the perfectly poised woman still had a job there.

"Welcome to City—" she started to chirp, until she recognized Kara. "Oh. Hello."

It wasn't an annoyed hello or a bored one. Rather, it was more curious.

"Hi," said Kara, placing another of the pink bakery boxes on the counter. "I brought this as an apology for getting you into trouble."

The information clerk's face lit up. "For me?" She tentatively peeked under the lid and gasped. "Éclairs. My favorite!" Ms. Binder's chair scraped against the floor as she pushed it back and hurried around to hug Kara. "Thank you. Nobody's ever done something this nice for me."

"You're welcome," said Kara. "I was also hoping to offer an apology to the mayor's assistant." She held out the other pink bakery box and let Ms. Binder see the contents.

"Well, I can't imagine she would object to a present," said Ms. Binder.

Kara nodded and waited.

Ms. Binder pointed to the elevators. "Elevators are right there, hon."

Kara took a step toward them. "You don't need to call and make sure it's OK for me to go up?"

"No," said the clerk, scoffing. "She's the mayor's assistant, not the mayor. And if she dares to try and have me fired, I'd love to see her use this as grounds."

There was a spark in Ms. Binder's eyes that hadn't been there before, and Kara could feel the conviction behind her words.

"What changed your mind from yesterday?" asked Kara.

The clerk smiled again and leaned forward confidentially. "After you left, I started working on my résumé. You know, thinking I might get fired. I was listing my skills, and I realized you were right. I *am* great at my job. If they don't want me here, there are plenty of people out there who will."

Kara beamed at the woman. "Absolutely!"

Things had turned out better with Ms. Binder than she'd expected.

Kara hoped it would be the same upstairs.

She clutched the last pink box to her and headed for the elevators.

The mayor's assistant was busy insulting someone on the phone, but as soon as Kara appeared, she hung up and jumped to her feet.

"You need to leave *now*," she told Kara.

Kara offered Courtney the pink bakery box, but Courtney sneered at it.

"You really think you can win me over with gluten? Get out!" She pointed down the hall.

"Actually," said Kara, opening the lid, "it's for your boss."

Courtney's jaw dropped, and she lowered her arm. "This is . . . the mayor loves this cake." She took the box from Kara. "But you can only get it in—"

"Central City," Kara finished for her.

Courtney breathed in the contents of the box. "It's fresh-baked! How did you do this?" She narrowed her eyes. "Is it fake? Is this a trick?"

Kara couldn't help laughing. "No. Let's just say the mayor isn't the only one with connections."

"Well, he'll be very happy to have this." Courtney closed the box and put it on her desk. "But as I'm sure you've heard, you've lost any interviewing privileges." She pointed at Kara. "You. Personally. No matter who you write for."

Kara nodded. "I'm not here to talk my way back into the mayor's good graces." She pointed to the bakery box. "The cake *is* for the mayor, but this apology is for you."

Kara adjusted her glasses and cleared her throat. "I am truly sorry I put you and the mayor in positions where you had no choice but to talk to me. You should always have a choice. Nobody should ever feel threatened for doing their job well, and"—Kara gestured at Courtney—"you are exceptional at yours. And so is he. I know you both want what's best for this city."

Courtney didn't speak or move. She just studied Kara.

"Well, that's all I have to say." Kara bounced on her toes. "Sorry again, and have a nice day." She gave Courtney a small wave and walked away.

"You still can't have that interview," Courtney told Kara.

"I know."

There was silence for a few beats, and then Courtney called, "But thank you for the cake."

Kara smiled as she pressed the elevator button. *That* was the Kara Danvers way of communicating.

Snapper wasn't as pleased with Kara as she was with herself. When she turned in her two articles, he smacked the pages with the back of his hand.

"Why are neither of these an interview with the mayor? Did you not apologize to his assistant?"

"I did," said Kara. "But I also told her I didn't want the interview."

Kara braced herself for an explosion from Snapper, but all he did was jut his lower jaw and thrust Kara's articles back in her hands.

"That wasn't your call to make, Ponytail," he said in a low, dangerous voice.

She fiddled with her glasses. "Actually, it . . . it was. A

good journalist knows when to broach a subject, and when to leave it alone." Kara shoved the articles back at Snapper, along with a plastic takeaway container. "Bear claw?"

"I hate bear claws," Snapper growled, but he dropped the articles on his desk and opened the container. "Explain yourself. Broach what subject?"

"I read your op-ed piece about physical books and libraries disappearing under the mayor's new initiative," said Kara. "I also know it's why he didn't want to talk to anyone from CatCo."

Snapper stared at her with half a bear claw wedged in one cheek. "Yeah? So?"

"So even if I got that interview, he'd want to spend it defending his digital library initiative. And, honestly, I don't think he's right. I think you are."

Kara expected her boss to smile smugly or gloat, but all Snapper did was shake his head.

"Journalists don't get to choose what stories to tell. Otherwise people accuse us of media bias." Snapper picked up the other half of the bear claw. "You need to get that interview."

Kara's first instinct was to disagree and storm off, but she thought about her conversation with Mon-El—about giving people what they wanted. Snapper seemed to be approaching the issue from a place of practicality. Maybe that was what he wanted from her, too.

"Chief, if all Mayor Lowell wants to talk about is his initiative, and I report on nothing but that, aren't I, in a way, supporting it?" she asked. "And isn't *that* media bias?"

Snapper tried to speak but his mouth was crammed with claw.

"And if I tell the mayor he *can't* talk about his initiative," she continued, "wouldn't that *also* be media bias?"

Snapper rolled his eyes and grunted.

Kara opened her arms wide. "It seems like we'd be in trouble for talking to him no matter what. Don't you think it's better to avoid the issue altogether and talk about something more interesting, like, say, a superbattle?"

Snapper finally swallowed and took a deep breath. But instead of commenting, he let out a long-suffering sigh and picked up Kara's articles. "Superbattle?"

"It's got several credible sources: the owner of the theater where the battle took place, the owner of a diner near the theater, the scientist who created the antidote, and the NCPD officer who made the arrests," said Kara, clasping and unclasping her hands.

Snapper scanned the article. "So these Dominants no longer have their powers?"

"Most of them don't," Kara corrected. "They depleted them during the superbattle."

Only two people had orichalcum-based powers left when the Dominants finally surrendered: Kara and Matt.

"What about the supercitizens who weren't in the fight?" asked Snapper.

"NCPD is tracking them to make sure they don't use their powers to cause trouble. *And* they've all received the antidote." Kara pointed to her article. "I mentioned it right here."

Snapper handed Kara the pages, covered in sticky fingerprints. "You put too many *r*'s in Supergirl's name. Unless she recently joined a punk band."

"But you'll take this piece in place of my interview with the mayor?" Kara asked hopefully.

Snapper leaned toward her and held up a finger. "Treasure this moment, because it will never come again. When I give assignments, I expect you to see things through to the end, no matter how you feel about them." He lowered his hand. "However, that interview was a minefield to begin with, and this piece on the superbattle . . . it isn't terrible." He glowered at her. "But if anyone hears of my mercy, I will fire you. Again. Loudly."

"I won't breathe a word," Kara said, doing her best not to grin from ear to ear. "And thank you."

"I swear, Danvers, my hair turns grayer every time I talk to you." Snapper shoved the rest of the bear claw in his mouth and walked away.

It was only when he was out of earshot that Kara threw her arms in the air and cheered.

"My writing isn't terrible!" She wrapped her arms around herself and squeezed.

At that moment, Kara didn't need her orichalcum super-power to understand what Snapper had been trying to say.

The meaning had made it through just fine.

# EPILOGUE

NATIONAL CITY MUSEUM WAS finally starting to look like its old self again.

*Or rather, like its* ancient *self again.* Fred the security guard chuckled at his own joke and checked his watch. Time to make the afternoon rounds.

A shaggy-haired college kid entered the Roman exhibit as Fred left. They nodded to one another.

"Hey, Fred."

"Good to see you, Marcus," said Fred, giving the kid a backward glance.

He'd heard Marcus had been one of those supercitizens

for a while—a strong one, at that—but had lost his power during a superbattle.

Fred clucked his tongue and ambled on to the next room. He didn't see Marcus reach past a velvet security rope to touch a recently repaired statue of Emperor Caligula.

"How's it going, Cal?" Marcus gave the statue a gentle pat, and it cracked along its original break lines, the head tumbling from Caligula's shoulders.

"Whoops!" Marcus reached out and caught the fifty-pound piece of marble.

On the tip of one finger.

Marcus smiled and gently placed the head back on Caligula's neck before moving on to the chipped bust of a woman.

Glancing around to make sure he was still alone, Marcus cradled the woman's cold marble face in his hands.

"Soon, my love. Soon we will be reunited," he whispered. "And this city? It shall be ours."

Children's laughter and voices came from the next hall over, and Marcus stepped away from the statue just as a dozen children ran into the room.

"Ancient Rome was the coolest!" a little boy said. "If I could be from any other time, I'd want it to be that one."

Marcus smiled to himself and strolled away.

*Child,* he thought, *be careful what you wish for.*

TO BE CONTINUED . . . .

# ACKNOWLEDGMENTS

Always, always, always thank you for family, friends, fans, and God.

For Barry Lyga, who is a walking library of superhero knowledge and led me to this dream.

For the team at Abrams Books, who have been ridiculously supportive and love Supergirl as much as I do.

For my agent, Jenn Laughran, who gets that I need to follow my heart.

For my parents, who raised an awesome nerd and have always encouraged whatever I endeavor.

For my big sis, who is always so proud of me.

For Eddy Delgado, who knows a lot about music and orchestra pits.

For the Rodriguez clan, who are the best in-laws a gal could ever have.

For my Lodge of Death girls, who overflow with love and support.

For Kami, Lisa, and Mandy, who have been there since the beginning.

For my Austin crew: Katie, Shayda, Jen, Amy, Carolina, Amanda, and Cecille, who bring sanity and humor to my life.

For Paula Yoo and Lisa Yee, who dispense their wisdom freely. And for the creators, writers, and cast of Supergirl, who make it so easy and fun to play in their world, including the team at Warner Bros. and the CW, including Greg Berlanti, Andrew Kreisberg, Todd Helbing, Sarah Schechter, Carl Ogawa, Lindsay Kiesel, Janice Aguilar-Herrero, Catherine Shin, Thomas Zellers, Kristen Chin, Josh Anderson, and Amy Weingartner.

El mayara.

# ABOUT THE AUTHOR

**JO WHITTEMORE** is the author of numerous fantasy and humor novels for kids, including: The Silverskin Legacy trilogy; *Me & Mom vs. the World*; the Confidentially Yours hexalogy; and *Lights, Music, Code!*, a series novel for Girls Who Code.

Jo is a member of SCBWI (the Society of Children's Book Writers and Illustrators) and is part of the Texas Sweethearts and Scoundrels. She loves to make people laugh; and when she isn't tickling strangers, Jo writes from a secret lair in Austin, Texas, which she shares with her husband.

THE ADVENTURE

CONTINUES IN

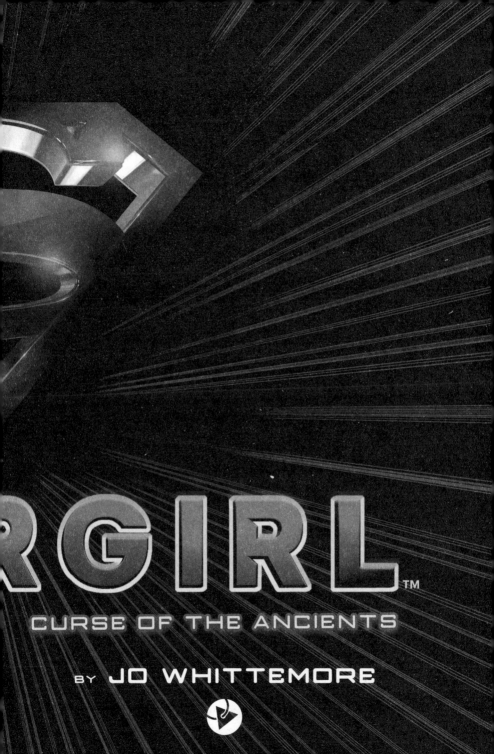

# RGIRL™

## CURSE OF THE ANCIENTS

BY JO WHITTEMORE

# 1

THE RUSTLE OF PAPER.

A soft cough.

And then . . . a violin's bow hummed across the A string.

Kara Danvers smiled as the sweet note pierced the near silence. A second later, the note grew into a melody that made emotion swell in her chest. If Kara's eyes hadn't been closed, everyone in Noonan's restaurant would have seen them fill with tears.

Just as swiftly as the music brought her down, it lifted Kara once more, and her smile returned, her cheeks forcing the tears to spill over.

The music stopped.

Kara opened her eyes.

"Miss Danvers, are you all right?" Hannah Nesmith, the curly-haired woman seated across from Kara reached out a hand.

"Oh, gosh, yes!" Kara laughed and removed the headphones she was wearing. "I'm so sorry. That was just . . . amazing." She removed her glasses, as well, and wiped her eyes with a napkin.

Hannah Nesmith was one of the few (too few, in Kara's opinion) famous female composers in the country. And Kara, who worked as a reporter for CatCo Worldwide Media, had been lucky enough to score an interview with her and hear one of her latest compositions.

Hannah smiled. "I'm glad you enjoyed it."

Kara passed the headphones and music player back to Hannah. "Seriously. I have never had a song *move* me like that!"

Hannah pointed at Kara. "You should hear it with a full orchestra."

"Oh, I don't think there'd be enough napkins," Kara said with a chuckle. "And bravo, by the way, for your skill on the violin." She clapped, and Hannah blushed.

"I actually play the flute in this piece; the person you just heard was Claude." As she said the name, Hannah's blush deepened.

Kara pursed her lips. "A good friend?" she asked with the innocence of someone pretending not to pry.

Hannah smirked at her. "You could say that. We play for the same orchestra, but we met during a triathlon."

Kara's jaw dropped. "Hold up! You're a ridiculously talented composer, musician, *and* triathlete?" She leaned toward Hannah and whispered, "Are *you* Supergirl?"

Hannah shrugged and laughed. "Maybe. She and I are never in the same place at the same time."

Kara laughed, too. *If only you knew you were sitting right across the table from her*, she thought.

Kara probed Hannah about her triathlon hobby, which had, in turn, led to Hannah's inventing an app for note-taking on the go. Kara flipped through the notes *she'd* just taken on a steno pad, shaking her head.

"Hannah, I would seriously kill for a fraction of your talent," she said.

"Oh, please. You and I aren't so different," Hannah said. "We're both writers who speak to people through our work."

Kara snorted. "Yeah, but *my* work doesn't sell out shows at National City Music Hall."

"But it could sell out a TED Talk," Hannah replied. "By this time next year, you could be in Vancouver, giving a speech on women in media."

Kara smiled. "I don't see myself ever going to Vancouver."

Their server arrived with the bill, and Kara plucked the check holder away before Hannah could reach it.

"Dinner is on CatCo," she said, even though she was pretty sure her boss, Snapper, would scoff at the idea. She'd once seen him drink from a coffee cup labeled ~~NO MORE~~ NEVER MR. NICE GUY.

Kara extended a hand to Hannah, who shook it. "This was such an honor, Ms. Nesmith. Thank you for meeting me so late in the day."

"Anytime," said Hannah. She leaned toward Kara. "And even though the performances are sold out, I've got VIP passes, so if you want to come with someone special . . ."

Kara smiled. Her someone special was Mon-El of Daxam, but his home world had been a party planet, where people were unlikely to listen to classical music. Anything without inappropriate lyrics was probably not going to be on his radar. Still, Mon-El had been spending a lot of time at National City Museum learning about ancient civilizations. Maybe Kara could convince him to expand his interests to classical music as well.

"I'd love to go," Kara told Hannah. "Thank you."

"I'll leave two tickets at Will Call," Hannah said. She glanced at her watch and grimaced. "I hate to eat and run, but I've got another appointment."

"Yes, go, go!" Kara waved her away and placed some money in the check holder.

Hannah smiled gratefully and rose from her chair,

colliding with a tall, sleek-haired brunette. Kara perked up when she realized it was one of her best friends, Lena Luthor.

"Oh! I'm terribly sorry. Are you all right?" Lena reached for Hannah's arm, and her eyes widened. "Hannah Nesmith! What are you doing here, of all places?"

"I just finished an interview with *CatCo* magazine," said Hannah, gesturing to Kara. "This is—"

Lena's face brightened. "Kara!" She opened her arms, and Kara stood and stepped into them, smiling.

"Hey, you! What are *you* doing here?"

They separated, and Lena nodded to a nearby table of suit-clad men and women. "I'm at a business dinner as well." In a lower voice, she added, "I'm hoping they'll fund a cancer cure I'm developing."

Hannah Nesmith laughed and shook her head. "Leave it to you to find a cure for cancer, Lena." She turned to Kara. "You want to talk talent? Back in school, Lena was a fencing master, a Chess Federation champ, *and* she finished two MIT Mystery Hunts in under twenty-four hours." She elbowed Lena. "But you left the coins for other people to find. So sweet."

Lena ducked her head. "You speak too kindly of me, Hannah." She squeezed her hands. "Are you in town for a bit?"

Hannah nodded. "I'm at the Wayward Arms if you want to catch up."

"I'd love that!" Lena's eyes flitted back to her table. "And now, I really must dash."

"Go get 'em!" Kara cheered.

Lena winked and hurried off.

"I'm afraid I have to go, too," Hannah told Kara. "If you have any more questions, please feel free to call." With a wave, she departed.

Kara watched both women walk away, visionaries and dynamos of the twenty-first century. Back when Kara had been Cat Grant's coffee-fetching assistant, Lena and Hannah had already been wowing the world with their talents.

The thought made Kara feel a bit . . . unimpressive.

Yes, she was Supergirl, but only because of Earth's yellow sun. And as Kara Danvers, she'd finally moved on from being an office assistant, but she was a barely recognized reporter.

Meanwhile, Hannah Nesmith was running triathlons, inventing apps, and composing symphonies, while Lena Luthor was mastering anything she even glanced at.

Neither Supergirl nor Kara Danvers could compare. But maybe she could change that.

Under the cover of darkness, Kara slipped into the alley behind Noonan's and leaped into the night sky. She soared over rows of buildings before touching down on the balcony of DEO headquarters.

The Department of Extra-Normal Operations was like her second home *and* office. Here, she worked for a Green Martian named J'onn J'onzz who posed as the human DEO director Hank Henshaw. His second-in-command was Kara's sister, Alex. But as Kara glanced around the control room, she didn't see either of them. She did, however, spot another one of her best friends, Winn Schott. He was sitting at his desk, a pen held between his upper lip and nose like a mustache while he tufted his dark hair and stared at a laptop screen.

"Hey, Winn?" Kara said as she approached him. "Have you seen J'onn or Alex?"

Winn let his pen fall into one hand and swiveled to face her. "Yeah, they're on the roof."

"The roof?"

"You know." Winn pointed up. "Big square thing above us that keeps the rain out."

Kara pinched his arm. "I know what a roof is, smartie. *Why* are they there?"

Winn grinned and squirmed out of her reach. "Apparently, there's a big comet coming. Dr. Hoshi brought her telescope, so everyone else is going to check it out."

Kara raised an eyebrow. "But you're not? Isn't this what you live for?"

When he wasn't inventing or hacking something, Winn was absorbed in science fiction and obsessed with outer space.

Winn scoffed. "Please. I've been to another planet *and* have the space rocks to prove it." He polished his fingernails on his shirt. "Once you've crossed the galaxy, everything else pales in comparison."

Kara smirked. "You're saying this to a girl who's crossed *several* galaxies."

Winn stared at her. "Let me have my moment, Kara."

She laughed. "Fine. But I still find it hard to believe you aren't interested in seeing the comet."

Winn shrugged. "It's orbiting Earth for five days, so I'll have plenty of chances to see it."

Kara crossed her arms.

He smiled sheepishly and pointed to his bag. "I may have a portable telescope I plan to break out later."

She nodded. "There we go. What are you working on now?" Kara started to turn his laptop in her direction, but Winn reached out and steadied it.

"Hey, hey, hey!" he said. "I'm doing some personal shopping."

Winn's cheeks turned pink.

"Are you buying more action figures, Winn?" Kara asked teasingly.

He shot her a look. "First of all, they're *collectibles.*

Second"—he turned his laptop so Kara could see the screen—"I'm buying a gift for Lyra."

Lyra, an alien refugee from Starhaven, was Winn's girlfriend. She was a bit of a wild child, but she had a good heart.

"Awww!" Kara squeezed Winn's shoulder and glanced at the screen. "That's ador . . . mat." She frowned. "That's a doormat, Winn."

He grinned at her. "Yeah, but look what it says." He enlarged the image, and Kara read.

"There's no place like 34.1546° N, 118.3340° W." Kara shook her head. "I don't get it."

"It's the latitude and longitude for my apartment!" Winn tapped his chest. "I'm giving Lyra a doormat for my home because I want it to be her home, too."

Kara gasped. "You're asking her to move in with you?" She squealed and bent to hug Winn. "That's great! And a *really* clever gift idea."

Winn leaned back in his chair and smiled smugly. "Just call me Mr. Terrific."

"Heh. Now I know a Mr. Terrific on *two* Earths." Kara glanced at the screen again. "Wait a minute. Winn? That doormat is a custom order." She clicked on a link. "And they aren't sure when it can be available."

Winn blinked at Kara. "Well, yeah. I didn't say I was ready for Lyra to move in *now*."

Kara rolled her eyes.

"Oh, don't judge me with your judging judgery." Winn waved a finger at Kara. "Lyra's out of town, and I miss her, so I'm keeping busy." He closed his laptop and slid it into his messenger bag. "That's why I'm about to meet James for patrol. You're welcome to join us."

"James" was James Olsen, one of her closest friends. He'd been sent to National City by Kara's cousin, Clark Kent, to watch over Kara before she became Supergirl. He now ran CatCo during the day and fought crime at night under the guise of Guardian, with Winn monitoring from a surveillance van.

"Thanks, but I need to talk to J'onn," Kara said, pointing up.

"If you change your mind, we'll be out all night." Winn stood and slung his bag over one shoulder. "You can find us at the corner of Danger and Excitement."

Winn walked away, whistling "Space Oddity," and Kara grinned. Then she zoomed out the balcony doors and up to the roof. Several uniformed DEO agents and one in a lab coat were gathered around a telescope; J'onn stood off to one side with Mon-El, Alex, and Alex's girlfriend, Maggie Sawyer.

At Kara's sudden appearance, the foursome stopped talking. J'onn, Mon-El, and Alex smiled, while Maggie stamped her foot and groaned.

"Aw, man!"

Alex held a hand out to her girlfriend, palm up. "That'll be five dollars."

Kara narrowed her eyes good-naturedly as the money changed hands. "Do I want to know what you were betting on?"

Mon-El raised his hands defensively and greeted Kara with a kiss. "For the record, babe, I didn't participate."

"Neither did I," said J'onn.

"We saw you flying toward the building," Alex explained to Kara. "Which, by the way, you should *not* be doing in your street clothes."

"I'd bet Alex that after you found out where we were, you wouldn't have any interest in joining us," said Maggie. "Because you've seen enough of space for a lifetime."

Maggie was one of the few people outside the DEO who knew that Kara was also Supergirl. The fact that Maggie worked for the National City police and had never revealed the secret made her an ally in Kara's book.

"And *I'd* bet that my little sister, who has the most curious mind in the universe, wouldn't miss seeing this comet for anything." Alex put an arm around Kara's shoulders. "And I was right."

Kara gave her sister an apologetic look. "Actually, I came to talk to J'onn."

Alex dropped her arm from Kara's shoulders, and Maggie let out a "Ha!" before snatching her five dollars back.

J'onn stepped closer to Kara. "You wanted to talk to me? What about?"

With Alex, Maggie, and Mon-El all listening, Kara blushed and adjusted her glasses.

"I was hoping I could start doing more for the DEO," she said quietly.

Mon-El smiled. "Doing more than protecting this city every day?"

Kara shook her head. "Not as Supergirl. As Kara Danvers."

"What?" Alex's forehead wrinkled in confusion, but Kara pressed on.

"I'm already familiar with a lot of alien species, but maybe I could specialize in something," Kara told J'onn. "Like alien weaponry. It would be good to know what I might face."

*Plus, it's definitely something Lena Luthor and Hannah Nesmith won't be experts at,* she thought.

J'onn stroked his chin. "We've got some artifacts in the subbasement you could look at, I suppose."

"That's a start," Kara said with a nod.

Alex nudged her. "Why are you going into DEOverdrive? Is everything OK at CatCo?"

"Of course." Kara gave her a reassuring smile. "I just want to . . . expand my interests."

*And be a little more impressive without my cape,* she added to herself.

"OK," said Alex, though she still looked puzzled.

"We can head downstairs after the comet appears," J'onn told Kara. He checked his watch. "Which should be any moment now."

J'onn beckoned for Mon-El, Maggie, and the Danvers sisters to follow him to the telescope, where the woman in the lab coat, Dr. Hoshi, was telling the other agents about the stars overhead at that moment. Normally, she acted as the DEO's physician. But tonight, the petite Japanese woman stood on tiptoe to point out a constellation.

"Want me to lift you a little higher?" Kara asked with a smile.

"Kara! Glad you could join us," Dr. Hoshi said in greeting. "And no, thank you. I prefer to keep my feet on the ground." She glanced down at the rooftop. "Or the concrete, in this case."

Kara gestured at the telescope. "I had no idea you were into astronomy."

"It's kind of my secret passion," Dr. Hoshi confessed. "Tonight, we're going to observe Caesar's Comet. Have you heard of it?"

"It was *not* named after the salad," Mon-El chimed in. "And if you suggest that, people will laugh." He cleared his throat. "A lot."

Kara held back a smile and rubbed his arm sympathetically. "I'm not familiar with the comet, Dr. Hoshi."

"It was last seen more than two thousand years ago, shortly after the death of Julius Caesar," the physician said. "Many Romans thought it was the deification of Caesar: proof that he'd become a god."

Dr. Hoshi turned to the rest of the group before she made her next comment. "It's also a daylight comet, which means it's bright enough to see during the day, but since it comes into orbit tonight, I thought it would be fun to witness its arrival."

She bent over the telescope and made a few adjustments before turning to her laptop.

"This is it!" Dr. Hoshi announced.

Everyone chattered excitedly and shuffled closer to the telescope.

"I'll adjust the telescope as the comet moves, but please don't linger too long, so everyone gets a chance to see it," she said. "While you're waiting, you should be able to see the comet with the naked eye right . . . there."

Kara glanced to where Dr. Hoshi was pointing and saw an ice-blue dot against the star-speckled darkness.

"Too cool," Alex whispered beside her.

Kara turned to answer but was blinded by a brilliant flash of light. All around her, people cried out in surprise.

The whole world had gone white.

Mon-El gripped one of Kara's hands, and she felt around for her sister with the other.

"Alex!" she cried.

"Kara!" Alex called.

Just as she touched her sister's fingers, a wave of energy slammed into Kara, knocking her hand loose from Mon-El's.

She felt herself falling.

Then everyone and everything went silent.

Before Kara hit the concrete, the white light faded to black, and she passed out.

# DON'T MISS THE EXCITING SECOND AND THIRD BOOKS IN THE SERIES!

# RACE INTO ACTION WITH